KING OF THE MALL

The Life And Loves Of A Hairstylist

Wolfe Armand Scarpati

Fiction inspired by actual events…

Copyright © 2019 Wolfe Armand Scarpati

ISBN: 978-1-64438-688-0

All rights reserved. No part of this publication may be reproduced, stored in a retrieval system, or transmitted in any form or by any means, electronic, mechanical, recording or otherwise, without the prior written permission of the author.

Published by Abuzz Press, St. Petersburg, Florida.

Printed on acid-free paper.

The characters and events in this book are fictitious but inspired by actual events. Any similarity to real persons, living or dead is coincidental and not intended by the author.

Library of Congress Cataloging in Publication Data
Scarpati, Wolfe Armand
King of the Mall by Wolfe Armand Scarpati
Fiction/Biographical | Romance | Erotica
Library of Congress Control Number: 2019903749

Abuzz Press
2019

First Edition

Dedication

To my family, who graciously accommodated me during the 2 years that it took me to write this book.

To my former peers and colleagues, many of whom were my mentors and inspiration over a 40-year career.

*To my Aunt Mary, whose words I will never forget:
"Always go to the big church..."*

...And finally, to all the women I have ever loved.

Foreword

The 70s and 80s were truly glorious times for the salon industry. So very many salons were located in malls; those sacred cathedrals of capitalism that saved suburbia from despair, and served as the bravura centerpiece for shopping, socializing, partaking in culinary delight *and,* if you worked there, *hooking up with the opposite sex.*

I was right in the middle of it all. I was in my mid-20s, getting ready to segue to age 30, and was the top hair stylist in one of the best salons in the suburban Philadelphia area. That salon was located in one of the large malls in the King of Prussia area. It was an area resplendent with several sizable malls, and people from throughout the Northeast flocked there to shop.

I had a natural talent for doing hair, I had *the look*, and I loved women. *God, I loved women.*

What better business to be in when you were as obsessed and preoccupied as much as I was with that one thing that gave me purpose for getting up in the morning...*getting laid*. It practically dictated my entire thought process all day long.

Working at the mall and being a hair stylist at such a well-known salon, I had access to tons of good-looking females, many of whom were willing, eager, and who looked at me as if I was some kind of a god...some kind of an idol. It was almost like being a rock star.

As for being blessed with *that look*, I knew how to use it to my best advantage both behind the chair in the salon *and* out in the clubs at night looking for my latest female conquest.

You just had to know how to pose, how to approach, and how to *sell yourself*, and in the end, it was *all about the sell.*

I was out every night after a 10 or 12-hour workday, with a stash of neatly folded bills in my pocket, the result of *cash* tips from a full day at the salon. Nobody used credit cards then. All the tips were cash.

When you were out in a nightclub or upscale bar, you set yourself up *to look a certain way,* and make yourself appear attractive and worthy. It was almost like a mating dance or a ritual; your back to the bar, elbows perched behind you, legs semi-crossed, and a somewhat serious demeanor on your face with brow slightly raised, *ala Burt*

Reynolds. You would take an occasional sip from your drink, but as you did, you were still continually scanning the nightclub or bar, and looking…looking for *that right one for that night*.

If by chance women were checking you out, you wanted them to think that you weren't just sexy, but also *quiet and mysterious*. It challenged them, and they approached you.

Pounding music usually pulsated to the point that you couldn't really carry on a conversation of any length even if you wanted to, but it didn't matter…that's not why you were there.

Out on the floor was *the night's menu*…a veritable buffet of great looking girls, and you had your pick, but…you also you had to think it out; observe before you made a move.

It was like a lion stalking a gazelle. I had it down to a science. I knew how to *get it done*.

There were the girls *that would* and the girls *that wouldn't*. Many of them were out for the same thing that you were. *Sex*. You just had to figure out who was who, and who was looking to hook up.

There were just as many females out on the hunt as there were guys like me. Pick the wrong one and you would probably be told to *fuck off*, regardless of how good looking you were….maybe they were already taken, or maybe they just weren't in the mood. Pick the right one and you were probably getting laid, or at the very least, getting a great blowjob out in the car that usually ended with the half-hearted promise of your giving them a phone call the next day, which of course never materialized…*after all, what did they think this was, serious?*

You see, the way it worked was that sometimes *they* thought that they had scored too. Maybe you saw them again, and maybe you didn't. If you *did* bump into them again it was usually from a distance at *another* smoke-filled club or bar, on *another* night, a week or two later. When they saw you, they would smile from across the room, and without a word spoken you knew if they wanted to *do it again*, or not. That's the way it was.

I, and others like me, were the Kings of the Mall. We got anything we wanted, we fucked anything wearing a short skirt or tight fitting pair of jeans, and as much as we wanted *them*, they wanted *us*.

There is however, a back story to all this, and it's not just about sex...it's about growing up in a small Northeastern coal mining town, the struggles that involved coming of age and growing up, and then finally escaping and leaving for life's pursuits.

King of the Mall is a fictional account that is based on *real events and real* people.....the names have been changed to protect the innocent, *and* the not so innocent....including myself.

The affairs that I had with all the women as depicted in the book, all happened, and in the end, my life ended up changing in a major way for so many different reasons.

The fact of the matter is that times change and *you change*. You mature, you grow older, and then come to the realization that you could only do it for so long. Long after it all ends, you mull it over; in my case for almost *four decades,* and then...*you write a book.*

My name is Wolfe Armand Scarpati, and this is my story.

Table of Contents

Chapter One - All American Boy 1

Chapter Two - 1973 – Dream Chaser 21

Chapter Three - 1974 / "The Perfect Girl" 33

Chapter Four - 1975 / The Move 44

Chapter Five - Demons 53

Chapter Six - Be Careful What You Wish For 63

Chapter Seven - Saint and Sinner 76

Chapter Eight - A Kind Of Normal 82

Chapter Nine - In The Midst Of Chaos 89

Chapter Ten - Adrianna 101

Chapter Eleven - 1983 - Meeka / New York 115

Chapter Twelve - An End, And A New Beginning 123

Chapter Thirteen - Tantra 134

Chapter Fourteen - Barbarians At The Gate 143

Chapter One
All American Boy

I grew up in Northeastern Pennsylvania; Pottsville. Pottsville was then, and still is, a small town sitting right in the center of Pennsylvania's anthracite coal mining area.

The town had a population of a little under 20,000 people during the mid-50s and throughout the late 60s when I was growing up. The majority of them were Italian, Polish, Irish, and predominantly Roman Catholic.

As you grew up in Pottsville, you ended up either loving it and embellishing yourself to its limited culture and way of doing things, or hating it, and then doing whatever you had to do, to get the hell out at some point.

That little city, and its ways and attitude either *owned you*, or it didn't. Sure, you always have a soft spot for that place that you call home, but you also know when it's time to leave.

My father worked in the strip mines and was up 6 days a week at 5:30 A.M. to get ready for another day of work. As a kid, more times than not, I was up before him, making his coffee in an old-fashioned silver steel percolator that was typical of every household in the 50s.

Dad always told me that if for some reason his alarm didn't go off, the aroma of the Maxwell House coffee I was brewing on our white ceramic and metal gas stove was the next best thing to wake him.

As he would come downstairs in the morning, resplendent in his long johns, he would say jokingly, and with a teasing smile on his face, *"Why the hell aren't you in bed like other kids, what're you doin' down here busting my balls for, so early in the morning?"*

His speaking to me in such an adult manner was not unusual. He was a tough, blue-collar, bold kind of guy, and in those days, father to son, and male to male, it was the way things were.

When I reflect back on it, really it was no big deal. We were raised *tough*, but with plenty of compassion behind it; perhaps the way it should be with kids today. There were no trophies for tenth place.

In those days, the whole process of being a parent had a different kind of candor and frankness to it, but all things said and done, we turned out ok because of it.

Truly, I think that all Dad wanted was his hour of solitude before he began his eight-hour shift in the strip mines as a maintenance man on the big earth moving power shovels. They had enormous bucket scoops on them; so big, in fact, that you could drive a Mack Truck inside of one, and park it. They were marvels of engineering, and some of them were twice the size of a standard two story three-bedroom house.

It was tough, laborious work, and he came home as black as the Ace of Spades. His only badge of honor for a day's work would then be eight hours' worth of anthracite coal dust, grease, and mud; sometimes all you saw were the whites of his eyes. Dad used to say that he put in a whole shift of what he called *"throwing blood."* I didn't understand it then. I understand it now.

Although I denied him of that much-needed solitude almost every morning, he tolerated it, and to some extent was amused by it, simply because that's what fathers do for their sons.

My mother worked for my Aunt Mary, who owned an upscale women's clothing store in town. My aunt was well off financially, and socialized with the elite of the area at the local country club, just a short drive up Interstate 81. Most of them were her clients. Her friends were from *old money*; they were the wives of coal barons, garment industry entrepreneurs, and insurance & real estate magnates. Her social circle consisted of the most affluent and wealthy people in our area, and as a family, we on many occasions benefited from those connections in more ways than just pure friendship. In Pottsville, being *connected* sometimes meant *everything*.

My mother, on the other hand, was the domestic one. More times than not, she was the glue that held the family together.

In the broadest of senses, Mom *did it all*; accountant, lawyer, counselor, gourmet cook, and advising elder sister to her siblings.

She hated people who watched daytime TV, and to her, you were just a *lazy son of a bitch* if you were not doing something worthwhile throughout the day if you happened to be a stay at home housewife that did not work.

Like all mothers, she *cried for you*, and *laughed with you*. I could fill a book with her wisdom and then write another one telling you of her tenacity. She didn't take any shit from anyone, but that's how the *Vacaro girls* were raised...*tough*. Mom had a saying..."*Don't eat the sausage, if you don't have the stomach to go into the kitchen and see how it's made.*"

Mom ran the house, worked part-time for my aunt, and Dad brought home the majority of the money. Strip mining, although it was a dirty, labor-intensive job, paid very well, thus she only had to work part time for my aunt. On the other hand, at home, she was like a *domestic CEO*, taking care of the house, as well as my brother and I. She was a budgeting genius, as everyone had to be in those days, took care of the the finances of the house, and the well being of the whole family. Together, my parents were a forged partnership that worked like a well-oiled machine for over 50 years prior to both their passing.

We came from a politically prominent family on my mother's side. My grandfather was a tough, second-generation Italian, who came up the hard way, picking slate on the coal banks as a 9-year-old youth forced to quit school in the third grade. Through diligent hard work, street smarts, and knowing how to play the game of life, much of it self-taught, he maneuvered himself into a prominent career involving both law enforcement and politics by the time he was in his early forties, and continuing until his death in 1967.

Because I grew up next door to my grandparents, I spent a tremendous amount of time with him; hunting, fishing, and doing carpentry projects around the house. We talked incessantly about baseball, it being a passion for the both of us. His influence on me still resonates today.

Being tutored in the ways of life by him was like being in Marine boot camp. There was *his way* or the highway, and it was not subject to negotiation.

I idolized him, and when he passed away in 1967 when I was 16, I cried. It made headlines in several local papers, and three ex-governors as well as a host of political dignitaries and prominent business people from around the entire state, attended his wake and funeral.

Aunt Mary, despite being well off, lived next door with my grandparents, and of course, took care of my grandmother after my grandfather died. She never left the homestead, however, because of her success in business she traveled the entire country as well as Europe for both work and leisure.

I guess you might say she was a happy spinster. She was content. Although she had been engaged at one time in the early 50s and broke it off, by the time she was forty years old, she could give a fuck less about ever getting married. For Aunt Mary, life was simply all about success, independence, having a buck in the bank, her family, and being able to come and go as she pleased. I think of her often.

When I was in my teens and on the verge of graduating from high school, she often spoke to me about getting out of the area, being smart enough to enter a high-paying field that might take me to Manhattan or the West Coast, and doing something that would eventually lead to notoriety. She thought that I would make a good fashion designer, because of my constant interest in my own wardrobe, and in men's clothing in general. I will always remember her for one phrase in particular: "Always go to the big church." Putting it in other words, what she was trying to tell me was to simply *get the hell out of here, and don't fuck around; take life, work, and money seriously.*

Much later in life, and in my career as a hair stylist, I was working for a top British owned salon in Manhattan, right on the corner of Fifth Avenue and 61st Street. I would often peer out of the floor to ceiling second floor window that was adjacent to where my salon work station was, look down at the sea of people walking below, and think of how proud she would be of me. I was in New York City, working with the best in my field, and I had *made it.* She passed away in 1974 and never got to see my eventual success. Undoubtedly, she would have been bursting with pride, I'm sure.

As a baby boomer growing up in the 50s and 60s, it was not unusual to live in a duplex, the other side of which was where your grandparents lived, or perhaps as we did, live one house over from them and have adjoining yards.

In the broad sense, there were no boundaries. Your life as a large family was very much filled with influences that stayed with you your whole life.

You walked into each other's houses unannounced, heard the occasional argument from next door in the summer when both the doors and screened windows were open, and mealtime consisted of not just the immediate family, but also at times the rest of the family from next door, if they happened to be there when either lunch or supper was ready to be served.

The whole food thing...the cooking, the sharing, the endless preparation that always seemed to be going on, was constant and essential, and at times the entire daily schedule completely revolved around it.

You could be rest assured that those circumstances were sure to generate many memories, as well as have long-term cause and effect that would undoubtedly be a major force in molding your personality, mindset, and tenacity for the rest of your life.

I had a reasonably normal childhood filled with the typical joys and troubles of growing up. In regards to childhood memories, most people have mental earmarks that define both the good times and the bad times.

You remember things by virtue of how old you were, or perhaps what grade of school you were in at a certain time. Your memories consist of happenings and conversations; in some cases remembering word for word, as well as circumstances; where you were, who you were with, who else was there, and what the outcome was, almost as if it had just happened yesterday.

Hopefully, in most cases and for most people, the good memories of youth and growing up outweigh the bad, but yet if there are any bad memories, they might somehow still occasionally come to the surface when thinking of those past times...even though you've tried to forget.

Let there be no doubt, every family fights, every family has problems, and every family has both good times and bad times.

In the end, if you aren't scarred or neurotic from any of it, can say that you generally had it good growing up, and can look at most of *what you perceived as bad times* as having been nothing more than nonsensical bullshit that really wasn't that bad after all, then certainly you came out ahead. I had it good. It wasn't perfect, but in hindsight, I can't complain.

I miss the simplicity of it all; at least, the *early* years of growing up. Looking back on things, it truly was simple. As a kid, you didn't know what a mortgage was, you didn't know what taxes were, and you had no idea of what the world political situation was. Perhaps from watching TV, you knew that the Russians were the *bad guys*, but that's all you knew. As a young adolescent boy, you are in many ways egocentric, in that your only concern was that which you were doing on any given day, as well as all of those things that to you were your most tangible of possessions...your baseball cards and Spalding baseball glove, your new Schwinn bike, your friends, and what was on TV that you didn't want to miss.

When you got up in the morning, you threw some water on your face, brushed your teeth, threw on a t-shirt and jeans, and started your day. Simple.

I played a lot of baseball, ran and played in the woods in the summer until it began to get dark outside, got into fights, and grew up in a neighborhood of kids that were then, and still are today, referred to as either *war babies* or *baby boomers*....those two niches of post-war newborns who where conceived from approximately 1945 through the very early 50s.

Our parents lived through World War 2, a mere decade or so previous, settled into a neighborhood where they would spend the rest of their lives, and in the process, they procreated.

It was a time of great prosperity. It was the beginning and development of American Pop Culture and Americana that became the hallmark of the 50s and 60s by way of music, fashion, fads, and culture.

Of course, those of us of a certain age remember the dark side of that era....the Cold War, the era of *duck and cover*, the Cuban Missile Crisis, and ultimately the fear of worst-case scenario....*that of being reduced to nuclear dust.*

Every time a TV program was interrupted with a black screen graphic that ominously screamed *News Bulletin* in bold white letters, you held your breath.

You knew everyone in the neighborhood, and were perhaps even distantly related. The one thing that rings true, both then and now, about Italian neighborhoods in particular, is that somewhere on the block, there usually lives a second, third, or maybe even a fourth cousin, and the way that you embellish each other is almost the same as if they are a brother or a sister. It has often been said that as a kid, your first best friends are often your cousins.

The several square blocks that were home to me, and which I played in, was humorously referred to in the area as *Nanny Goat Hill*. The original Italian immigrants who settled there in the early part of the century, did indeed raise goats in the Italian tradition. Although that era was long gone, the name stuck. The particular neighborhood that I lived in was resplendent with family, as well as neighbors whom you became close to and knew your whole life until they passed away.

They would watch over all the kids in the neighborhood when circumstances warranted it, and had the liberty of acting as parent to some degree, doling out an occasional scolding when it was called for to a gang of us for our rowdy, noisy, and sometimes bullish behavior. That, in turn, caused you the gut wrenching angst of worrying about whether they were going to tell Mom and Dad about what went on. If 24 hours went by and nothing was said, you were probably safe.

A gang of us from the neighborhood started elementary school together, beginning with kindergarten, and on through the sixth grade. We all walked to the same small elementary school one block away; something almost unheard of today. They were happy times, but let there be no doubt, it was also a time of pecking order being established, based on any number of things. Those times would further define your next few years of adolescence, as well as those years leading into your early and mid-teens.

In looking back on it now, most of it was nothing more than youthful fodder, but you somehow can't understate the importance of it.

Without question, those years were singularly *the* most important factor as to the confidence level you developed, how you carried yourself, and perhaps even the tenacity, or lack of, with which you eventually tackled life and all of the shit that was about to be thrown at you. After you were handed a high school diploma, you got a *job well done* pat on the back, and a *welcome to the real world* kick in the ass that comes with finally entering true adulthood.

I think those formative years, although important for both sexes, are especially trying for a young boy of 12 or 13. They were so, for a precocious little shit like me, who loved attention and developed a yearning for the opposite sex by the time of my first sixth-grade dance.

Growing up happens in a heartbeat. One day you're in diapers, and the next day you're trying to figure out *why your dick is getting hard* and what to do about it.

Junior high school was especially tough for me, and I experienced the typical problems that one goes through in not only entering your teen years, but also entering a whole new school environment.

At the age of 13, you're not a kid any more, yet parental protocol requires that you still be treated like one. For me, there were the endless battles that revolved around my first yearnings for a little bit of freedom and trust, as well as simply not wanting to be treated like a child anymore.

Combine that with hormones running wild, mixed up emotions that accompany the onset of adolescence, as well as overall peer pressure, and it's like a small nuclear bomb ready to go off.

You're still too young for a job, dependent on your parents for a buck or two spending money...maybe a small stipend of an allowance for chores done...and by that time, all kinds of crazy shit is going through your head. You drove yourself crazy, and, your parents along with you.

You started to become *aware*, and most of it involved things that just a few short years ago you could give a fuck less about; aware of clothing, aware of the way you looked, aware of music and trends, and, *aware of the opposite sex*.

Let there be no doubt that the latter revolves around the very beginnings of sexual drive and lust as well. You may not have realized it then...you probably just couldn't figure out why you were getting that dizzy, anxious feeling in your head, as well as a knot in your stomach when you were around certain females of the same age. In a short span of about 24 months, from ages 11 to 13, you go from *baseball* to *blue balls*.

There was usually someone in the neighborhood gang, or perhaps an older brother of someone in the gang...*someone who was just a bit older and more mature*, who told you what to do with that *hard thing* between your legs. Maybe you simply read about it somewhere, *or* perhaps saw it on a lavatory wall, and jaw dropping as it may have been when you first found out, tried to get a grasp on it.

In my case, my seventh grade best friend, Robert, salaciously explained the whole thing to me on our long 10-block walk to the junior high school on a cold winter morning. *You do what? You put it where? You must be fucking kidding me.*

From that point on, I knew what to do, I just didn't stand a snowball's chance in hell of doing it with anyone, and even if I did, it wouldn't have lasted all of 3 seconds.

Remember, this was 1964, and seventh-grade girls were those from a much simpler and much more innocent time. As a *seventh-grade boy*, you ended up fantasizing a lot, and *taking care of it in whatever way you had to.*

Without a doubt, young girls of that age and from that era were certainly going through the same physical, mental, and biological metamorphosis that we as boys were, but in 1964 there were just too many barriers and social morays. The whole societal thought process was radically different, and in many ways kids just grew up *slower*, with far less outside influences to hasten the growing up process, as compared to today.

At that age, the initial blooming of interest in the opposite sex was usually limited to, and revolved around, the classroom gossip of *who likes who.*

In a somewhat cute but humorous way, your classmates would joke about who was *boyfriend and girlfriend*, and as a result, the usual course of events involved you practically bribing someone in your class to casually inquire, and *find out if she likes me or not.*

If you were lucky, you mustered up enough balls to ask *that chosen one* to dance at the Fall Fling, and then walk her home. The result, after saying an awkward good night, was usually a quick run home for one hell of a session that probably included one of your older brother's *Playboy magazines* held in a secret stash; that holy of holiest places that your mother didn't know about, and thus was not capable of snooping in.

It's funny how I could always come home from a school dance, and in my mind put a certain female classmate's face on a mature, airbrushed, naked, female body in a magazine.

As a seventh or eighth grader struggling with constant female rebuffing, and wondering when the hell things will turn right for you, there were always the ones you heard about...*the advanced girls.*

They were usually the ones who started to develop physically much earlier than the other girls did, were two years older than you were, were in the ninth grade, and had already been *dating* for a year or two. They were also usually the substance of rumor, based on the hearsay that they were going out with a senior high school guy.

Surely, they were 'putting out'...or at the very least, if they weren't having sex, they were being *very generous in allowing roaming hands, or maybe even doling out hand jobs.*

You simply didn't stand a chance against a senior high guy; they drove, and you didn't. They were probably a foot taller than you were, lettered in sports, and most likely, were able to get beer too.

By tenth grade and somewhere close to the approach of your sixteenth birthday, your parents were asking *tongue in cheek* if you have a girlfriend. Perhaps it was to make light banter at the dinner table, but then again, perhaps it was to make sure that you weren't *gay*....to make sure that *all you were exposed to* in those first crucial 15 or 16 years; the upbringing, the importance of family, *the whole Catholic thing*, did its job and that you turned out *right*...in their eyes, making sure that you turned out to be *The All American Boy.*

The whole gay thing wasn't talked about except in private corners of conversation and gossip. In those days, *the closet* held more than brooms and coats. It was a different time and a different mentality, especially in a staunchly Roman Catholic Italian American family.

Gay rights as we know them today did not exist, and the whole liberal thought process of a *brave new world of hope, equality and communal solidarity* didn't seriously have its beginnings until 1967, the so-called *Summer of Love.*

1967 was not just the beginning of my sophomore year in high school; it was also the beginning of a whole new social life for me, and in many ways, it was a release of the shackles and chains of junior high angst and uncertainty.

Something clicked for me. Maybe I thought I was hot shit now that I was in high school, maybe I had just matured more, or maybe it was the joy of finally being treated a little more like a grown-up.

The next several years, up until my high school graduation in 1969, were nothing short of a whirlwind.

You find out a lot about yourself in high school, and in the broad sense, you get your first taste of what it's like to be an adult. Much of what is ahead for you in both *life and love* can be learned in high school, but the problem is that you're just *too fucking stupid* to pay attention to what's happening, and grasp the fact that the microcosm of over a thousand dizzy-ass teenagers under one roof is really the best training ground for everything that lies ahead of you in life.

Comparatively speaking, that pecking order that I spoke of earlier was mere child's play, compared to the dynamics of the high school social order, which itself was truly a full-blown universe that consisted of kings, queens, commoners….*and assholes.*

You very quickly found out who's who, and what it took to make a position for yourself that at the very least *would not* relegate you to the latter category… *God, let me be something, anything, but please don't let me get labeled as an asshole.* The odds of getting your first feel of warm pussy then *surely* goes down exponentially.

You experience quite a bit during those several years of high school. There are times when you have victories, and there are times when you have defeats; perhaps getting your heart stomped on by the object of your affection, or getting a rock hard erection deflated by the object of your lust who sat next to you in Geometry class, was totally out of your league, and would have absolutely nothing to do with you.

Sometimes it seemed as though the *popular ones,* indeed, *the good-looking ones,* were from a completely different planet, and in many ways were untouchable and beyond your reach.

You went out, you dated a bit, and you hung out downtown on hot summer nights when the humidity was thick and the sexual tension that was created from the sight of sweet young things in their newly fashionable mini skirts was enough to send you into a fantasizing frenzy.

I had a few serious girlfriends over the course of three years in high school; nice girls, the kind that your friends respected. The last thing that you wanted was an intervention where a few of your buddies cornered you and said, *"What the fuck are you doing with that skank?"* Mind you, *that was ok*, if it involved *a roving night out with the boys* to see what girls you could pick up downtown, but, above and beyond that, you chose *a girlfriend* far more carefully, and with entirely different criteria to go by.

Even if your friends knew that you were dating a *nice girl*, you still might be asked if you were *getting any,* so you had three choices…not answer, change the subject, or lie. If you lied, you never carried it too far; *Yeah, she has great tits, and they're everything I expected*; end of story; *don't ask me anything else, and don't force me to lie more*. After all, she was your girlfriend, thus lines had to be drawn in the sand, even when the questions came from your best friends.

In light of the fact that the sexual revolution in 1967-68 was already well underway, it, as well as the explosive social and political revolution that was occurring elsewhere in the country, had not yet hit Pottsville in any profound way. We were simply too busy running around in our cuffed pants and penny loafers, listening to Motown, having our hair shorn bi-weekly, and trying to live up to our parents' expectations.

Most of us had not had sex yet, and surely for the few that did, it was with reckless abandon and lack of any skill. There was no thought process to it. You put your dick in, you got off, and that was the end of it. The thought of giving a female any pleasure, or making her eyes roll back in her head, wasn't even in the equation.

During our senior year, there were three girls in the class that got pregnant prior to the end of the school year. One of them, a Jewish girl from a wealthy family, got whisked away to Florida to finish out the school year, by her well to do parents.

As for the others, one stuck it out, had the baby, and became a very young single mother with the help of supportive parents, and the third got married almost immediately after graduation, thereby lending a degree of legitimacy to the whole thing.

When you heard about it, you were in some ways stunned, simply because you knew the girls, or perhaps had classes with them...maybe you even lusted over one of them, as hopeless as it might have been, since she was already taken.

Jesus Christ, he was fucking her all along? And here I am, like a goddamn jackass, sitting next to her in class, thinking about what it would be like to just be with her, cop some titty, and maybe, feel the real deal down below.

As my senior year ended and the summer of '69 loomed ahead, I faced a great deal of uncertainty. I had initially thought about following in my older brother's footsteps and joining the Navy, but that thought was stopped dead in its tracks by an avalanche of influences, change, and self-awareness that I was going through, and would, unbeknownst to me, set the course for me for the rest of my life.

Pottsville itself was going through some profound changes as well; you saw it in the streets, and almost everywhere that you went.

The way that both men and women dressed was changing radically, and was becoming more liberal and fashionable. You finally started to see longer hair on guys, a trend which came late to the area, but which was finally in full bloom by that summer.

Even my blue-collar, ultra conservative father began to sport somewhat longer hair, in addition to growing long thick silver sideburns. He loved it when women would tell him that he looked like the actor, Lorne Greene, who starred in the TV western, *Bonanza.*

Bare midriffs and tight bell-bottomed jeans were *de rigueur* for most young females, and the sight was enough to make you crazy, as you followed them on the street from behind, just to catch a glimpse of a great looking ass moving back and forth, silhouetted by tight blue denim.

Independent clothing stores, or *boutiques* as they were called, sold the latest fashion-wear for both sexes and were popping up throughout the downtown area. A new word entered out language...*unisex;* It became the operative word for clothing and hair, as it applied to both sexes.

In our area, night clubs and bars were opening up that featured live rock bands. Most of the top bands came from as far away as Watertown, New York and their influence spawned a legion of loyal followers. That, in turn, dictated which night spot the *over-21 crowd* went out to on any given night of the week. You always watched the ads that were on the back page of the newspaper to see *what band was playing where*, and that then dictated your night out and where you went.

As this was long before the era of photo driver's licenses, and the drinking age in Pennsylvania was 21, at ages of either 18, 19, or 20, you did whatever you had to do to get fake ID cards. That, in turn, would give you an *'in'* to the nightclubs and bars, and you could then hang out with an older, hipper crowd. Even at the age of 20, you felt as though you were still in a *not of legal age limbo*. It seemed as though finally turning the age of 21, and then having the freedom to get into any nightclub or bar, would never come.

You wanted in; you wanted to be part of it; *everyone that age wanted to be a part of it*.

The *Hippie Movement* had, to some degree, finally made its way to the area, and on the nights that the downtown area was open late, the once quiet avenues of retail were jammed with crowds of cocky young rebels with shoulder-length hair, accompanied by barefoot girls in long flower-patterned skirts that were embellished with the scantiest of tube tops.

The police were omnipresent, ready to move along the vagabond groups, nay *the flower children,* that were hanging out downtown, and who were congregating in front of the entranceways to stores. The police would then swoop down and charge them with loitering. The tension between the generations was at times nothing short of hostile.

Drug arrests for marijuana, as well as other recreational drugs of choice, were finally starting to make headlines in all of the local newspapers, even for minor infractions that by today's standards would barely be worthy of a paragraph devoted to, on the back page.

It was truly a summer of awakening and independence for me, and with that awakening came the battles with parents; battles over staying out late, who I was hanging out with, how I looked and dressed, and most of all, what I was going to do with my life.

I had started to grow facial hair in the form of a big floppy mustache, as well as having let my hair begin to grow long. My mother was convinced that I was on my way to a life of drug-ridden depravity, reprehensible morals, and being homeless out on the street, all because I had started to grow my hair longer, and eventually wear it in a ponytail. The arguments were endless, and on a daily basis.

Later that summer, as the Manson Murders unfolded, and Charlie and his merry band of females were on the news almost nightly, she, along with my father, would just gaze at the evening news on the TV in complete horror, talk about how the world was going to *hell in a handbasket*, and blame our entire generation for all the woes that beset the country not just in 1969, but for several years previous as well.

Somehow The Beatles even got dragged into it. My father hated them. *"Bastards...they started all this shit..."* In his mind, they were responsible the downfall of an entire generation, and that feeling was further compounded when it came out on the news that Manson and crew had sprawled the words from one of the Beatles' songs, *Helter Skelter*, in bloody regale on the walls of that horrible, suburban Hollywood murder scene. He blamed them for everything.

One of the main reasons I ended up not joining the Navy was simply the fact that I was absolutely horrified at the thought of having my head shaved in boot camp, and then being relegated to 4 years of military regimented super short hair.

Really, on a somewhat subliminal level, it was a sex thing; *how the hell was I supposed to get laid looking like that?*

Facts being facts, the *hip* crowd looked a certain way, and dressed a certain way. All the young girls were just crazy over a good-looking guy with great looking long hair. Moreover, the whole hair thing was so connected to, and played such an important part in, the rest of the look...the clothes, the swagger...the whole package. You needed to have stylish long hair in order to meld the whole thing together, and play the whole role.

There were other reasons as well. After 12 years of relative anonymity in school, marginally making it to the realm of only modest popularity, and after having had only moderate success with the opposite sex, I was hell bent on getting noticed…hell-bent on *them*, the females that at one time had spurned me, saying to themselves, *wow, didn't he fucking change…let me just drop my pants right now*; as if that little fantasy was ever going to happen.

No…no Navy for me. Fuck that shit, I'll figure something else out.

The summer of 1969 was memorable for a lot of reasons. Neil Armstrong walked on The Moon, the Woodstock Music Fest happened, Manson's Hollywood murders, Kennedy's Chappaquiddick incident, and for me, the first time I had sex…if you could call it that.

It was about as awkward as awkward could get, and it was indeed the night that Neil Armstrong walked on The Moon, thereby attributing as to why I remember the exact date.

Now, think about this for a moment…most people, be they male or female, remember without fail their *first time*; who it was, where it was, and perhaps some other ancillary details that make that so called *special night* unforgettable. Truly, barring its having happened on a birthday or prom night, the odds of them knowing or remembering *the exact date* of when it happened are almost nil.

On July 20th, 1969, Neil Armstrong became the first human to set foot on The Moon less than six hours after having landed, and I, in turn, got my first euphoric feel of finally putting my dick in wet pussy, *less than one hour* after having set foot into a seedy under-21 basement night club called The Lower Level, which was just up Interstate 81 in the neighboring city of Hazleton. In some ways, I remember so much, yet in other ways the years have clouded my mind.

I remember her by her first name only; Maryanne. I can recall standing with the crowd watching the band and then striking up a conversation with her; but most of all, I remember her low slung jeans, bare midriff with tan skin, tight ass, and the smell of Heliotrope vanilla fragrance that spiraled around my head as she flirted with me and I flirted back, instantly giving me an erection that I could have broken through a brick wall with.

My friend Mike and I drove up to Hazleton that night. Mike had a car, and I didn't. Taking a quick break from my conversation with her to find him in the crowd, I begged him for his car keys, explaining the circumstances, and what I possibly had going on.

I remember stealthily leaving the club with her, her arm wrapped around my waist, she saying to me *"Oh my God, you're so skinny, you're so cute..."*, as we slowly walked out to Mike's car at the very far end of the dark parking lot, almost by itself. Beyond that, it's a bit of a blur, yet I recall some of the more prominent moments.

I can remember that it was hot as hell that night. Once we made our way to the car, there was a quick make-out session, consisting of the usual *accouterment* of car fucking foreplay; tongue in mouth, hands all over each other, pants being pulled down, dick in, and then, about 30 seconds later, it was over....no condom, a bit of small talk afterward, getting ourselves put back together again, and exiting the car as if nothing had ever happened. As crazy as it seems, of all the dizzy-ass things to enter my mind after having accomplished what for me was nothing short of a monumental feat on that *night of nights*, I remember thinking to myself, *Christ, it's almost 9:30, I wonder if the astronauts got out and walked on the moon yet; I hope it doesn't happen until I get home later.*

After walking her back into the club, we went in two different directions; a slow release of sweaty hands as we separated, and a beautiful smile on her face. She quietly mouthed an innocent *goodbye* to me, saying she was going to find her friends, and kissed me on the cheek. With that, it was over. It was done. *History.*

By that time, the place was packed, and I made my way back through the smoke-filled crowd, found Mike to give him back his car keys, and hoped that by the time I got home later, I wouldn't have missed any of *the rest of that historic night* on the TV. Maybe NASA and Walter Cronkite would wait specifically until I got home.

I never saw her again. I never knew her last name, and today I wonder where she is.

That summer the Viet Nam War was still in full swing, and so was the military draft. My parents, like countless other parents of the time, were worried sick that I would be drafted into the army, and end up in Viet Nam...especially my mother.

I had decided to not join the Navy, which at the time was considered to be a *safe* choice of the military, as opposed to being drafted into the Army, sent to Viet Nam, and thus, possibly ending up in a flag draped casket. I acquiesced to my parent's wishes, and enrolled for the upcoming fall semester at the local community college, located up in Wilkes-Barre. I made the registration for school with just days to spare until the deadline for signing up.

Really, the whole thing was a cop-out. I had graduated from high school by the absolute skin of my balls, had no idea what I wanted to do, and the equation was quite simple...go to college in order to get a draft deferment and you're safe...don't go to college, and then you have to pray that you *didn't* get a low number in the monthly draft lottery, which in turn, would have you getting called up to report for an army physical in less than 30 days.

I wasn't the only one relegated to those slim life choices. A few of my friends were in the same situation that I was, and were also attending the same community college, for the very same reasons...to avoid a world of green camouflage fatigues and barking drill sergeants.

I hadn't seen too much of them that summer, as they had gone down to the Jersey Shore to work, and only came home on occasional weekends. By the time the end of summer came, and they returned in late August to start school, it became very obvious to me that the four of them had been exposed to far more life maturing and personality changing events than I had. I subsequently found that out, when riding with them up to the college on the days that our schedules meshed. Bob, Pete, Rich, and Albie had, in plain words, turned into *four crazy bastards*.

Maybe it was that summer down at the Jersey Shore, where I'm sure they partook in all the debauchery that one would expect would accompany a summer of free reign, half naked-girls roaming the beach, the availability of alcohol, *tons of weed*, and no parental oversight.

By the time I saw them again when the end of August finally came, it was as if those 3 months down at the Jersey Shore had begat them 10 years of added maturity.

Undoubtedly, I had quite a bit of catching up to do. In due course, riding back and forth to school with these lunatics 4 days a week, it didn't take long. The conversation on the way up and back was usually the same every day: *where could we score more weed, who's skipping class to go down to the war rally down on the square, and "Hey man, I heard that chick, Suzy, got so high last night she fucked four guys at the party at Guthrie's house."*

Crazy bastards indeed…riding up Interstate 81 in Bob's metallic blue 1964 Chevy, doing 70 miles an hour in a 50 mile per hour zone, eight-track stereo blasting *The James Gang* with the windows down, and a huge bag of weed on Rich's lap, he then rolling joints to pass around; they could give a fuck less if they saw a state police car parked on the side of the road. It was as if they were sending out a dare, but somehow by the grace of God, we never got caught.

For the most part, I was petrified, yet somehow, in some strange way, I was also excited by the danger of it all.

The music of the era was incredibly important to everything we thought, did, and felt.

If there was any one thing that defined us in 1969, it was *the music*. Rock and Roll became simply, *Rock.* Even in lieu of the new portability of eight-track audio tapes, vinyl records were still state of the art for recording, and, that which you collected. You no longer just collected single records called *45s*; you purchased and collected *albums*…Bob Dylan, Crosby Stills and Nash, The Beatles, The Stones, Grand Funk Railroad, and many more idols of the time.

You embellished it, you wrapped yourself around it, and in some ways, it was almost as if the music, the bands, and your album collection was very much a central character in your everyday life.

Social media didn't exist then, nor did the rants, raves, fake political news, egotistical opinion, and selfies, that accompany it today. At that time, and in that era, the music became, and acted as, the social media of the day. It was a conduit for an entire generation to have a voice and to rebel. It was a major part of your life at that age, and the influence that it rendered prompted you to dream of a possible lifestyle which, for most of us, was unobtainable.

We talked about the bands incessantly, and what it must be like; big money, lots of women, the touring, and the lifestyle. Hell, fuck all this college shit, I wanted to be in a band. *We all wanted to be in a band.* I lasted less than a year in college and quit.

Eventually, I made one more half-hearted attempt at it a year later, for no reason other than to simply appease my parents, and once again to continue to avoid the draft by virtue of being a full time college student, thereby having a draft deferment. It was all to no avail. I just didn't have it in me. I was far too preoccupied, and my head was, in plain words, up my ass.

At that point, having left college, I still had my dreams. I just didn't quite know what to do in order to obtain the lifestyle that I yearned for.

Over the next several years, I fell into a succession of meaningless jobs, and was just spinning my wheels.

What I didn't know, was that eventually, it was all about to change.

Chapter Two
1973 – Dream Chaser

By 1973, I had been out of high school almost four years, and was 22 years old.

Things on the job front were not good, and did not appear to be getting any better. I just couldn't find anything that I wanted to do, and was completely immersed in things that were anything but positive in regards to having some type of viable career, becoming financially independent, and thus turning into what might be termed *a responsible adult*.

I was still living with my parents, was going through a succession of mediocre jobs, and was about as frustrated as one could be. The routine became mundane and boring; get up, go to work, come home, eat supper, take a shower, and then go to one of the local bars for a couple of hours. Depending on who I was hanging out with, maybe we would smoke some weed, or blow a little coke. I had discovered drugs, and the solace that they provided me with.

I didn't do much cocaine. It was a great high, but it gave you way too much in the way of *balls*. You became overconfident to the point that you were just a bit out of control, and thus more likely to get your ass kicked, which someone of my small stature of just under 5'6" and barely 110 pounds soaking wet couldn't afford to chance, so I basically stuck with the mellow high that one gets from weed, and occasionally a little hashish.

It was a repetitive cycle which I hated, and I was well aware of my parents' disappointment in me. Both of my parents certainly expected a lot more from me by that age, or at least for me to have some type of a life plan by that time that would bear fruit.

The arguments with my mother and father over things such as how long my hair was, or how I looked and dressed, were long over. They had, for the most part, acquiesced themselves as to how I was, and were all too happy with the fact that at the very least I kept my nose clean, stayed out of trouble, and was generally compliant to their way of doing things while I was living under their roof.

I had, by this time, bought my first car, a burgundy MG Midget convertible with British flags on both of the side doors and front hood, and which further became one of *the recognizable sets of wheels in town* as it cruised up and down the main drag of Pottsville.

There's something about a distinctive car like that in a small town; without question, it gives you recognition, and in many ways says *who you are, and what you're all about*. Onlookers would see that car coming and they would immediately know that it was me. *I was somebody*. I loved every minute of it. It was a *chick magnet*, and I loved the attention and the stares.

Generally speaking, as bleak as things were, the only solace that I had was the car, being able to look forward to going out with my friends at night, and the fact that I had finally developed *my style...my look*, as well as now having enough confidence to approach just about any female that I had an attraction to. I had balls the size of cantaloupes when it came to girls.

In my penis-driven little 22-year-old brain, I had absolutely no problem with putting the moves on any sweet young thing that I deemed to be approachable, and, *fuckable*.

I wasn't a 70s version of any of these guys that you *currently* read of and hear about, and who by today's standards and news events are the focus of the *'Me Too Movement'*...not by any stretch; let me make that perfectly clear. I *never* forced myself on anyone, and after all, this was the 70s...the era when use of the birth control pill had really come into its own. Most single young girls were indeed on the pill. The sexual revolution that started in the 60s was still very much in full swing. Everyone was on the make. Everyone was fucking. There was a whole new take on sexual morality. It was as simple as that. The bars and nightclubs were a veritable smorgasbord of lust for *both* sexes.

As well, the sexual freedom of the day was compounded by what one might call a *safety valve*, if you will; a few shots of penicillin was the only price to pay for a lifestyle of rampant and available sex. If you contracted a venereal disease, it could be easily dealt with. Hopefully, your family physician would shoot you up, keep his damn mouth shut, respect the whole confidentiality thing, and *not tell your parents*, even though he, in all likelihood, delivered you and all of your siblings at birth, and had probably treated the whole family for their ailments for 20 years plus. It was especially true in regards to our family physician, who had become quite a close family friend over the years. I could vividly remember my father bringing him fresh green romaine lettuce and tomatoes from our home garden whenever he went in for a checkup, or an office visit for some minor malady.

AIDS didn't exist at that time, and the thought of death as a possible consequence of getting laid never entered my mind, or anyone else. It would be another ten years and well into another decade before we would even begin to hear of the life-threatening HIV virus and AIDS.

I always knew which women I wanted, and used my newfound prowess and newly developed looks to go after the opposite sex with every bit of charm and tenacity I could muster. I loved dark haired girls with dark eyes…tiny, tan, and the smaller the better. Five feet tall for me was a dream come true; gorgeous little feet with painted nails, low slung bellbottoms that showed off a bare midriff, and a well-shaped belly button that just gave a hint of the paradise that was waiting below.

I was really in my element in the summertime. The clothing was skimpy, and the sight of tan legs and a tight ass in clingy blue jean shorts cut high on the leg was enough to put you through the roof.

I really had a thing for tiny girls. It was a *power fuck* thing…the smaller they were, the bigger your dick looked relative to they being so much smaller than you, even for a guy like me who was of average size.

You fucked like a jackhammer, and being somewhat physically bigger than they were made you feel invincible. You always walked away feeling like you gave them *the best they ever had*…whether that was true or not was another thing entirely, but when you were done you usually had an ego the size of Montana.

Maybe it was me, or maybe it was just the morally casual swank of the 70s that to some degree made getting laid fairly easy, unless of course, you were a walking talking disaster; but I was usually racking up notches on my belt on a weekly basis, sometimes not. If you *didn't* get laid, you simply went home and told yourself there was always the next time…and there *usually was a next time*.

I finally did get drafted, and received a notice to report for an army physical. My not being in college anymore, and no longer having the coveted 1A student deferment had its consequences. In my case, my birth date of March the 14th came up low in the spring draft lottery, as number 53. It was like being a marked man, and the handwriting was on the wall.

I received my notice to report for an Army physical at the Wilkes-Barre testing and induction center within 30 days of the draft lottery.

I can remember the look of pure worry on my mother's face; that look of dread that also was a look of premonition. Mothers have a way of doing that. When they are worried about something, it's usually because they have this uncanny motherly instinct which allows them to visualize things in multiple steps...the long term, the last of which is *worse-case scenario.*

It usually starts with that which is happening now and is simply not good, segues to that which could get far worse, and then ultimately the possibility of that *act of God* which brings tears, changes life entirely, and which one must accept as a *good Catholic* who does not question the motives of *the lord, thy God above.*

In Mom's mind, I was definitely headed into the army, and I'm sure she was convinced that I would be be coming home in a rectangular metal box with a flag draped over it.

Knowing her as I did though, there was probably a counter rationale to all that; a rationalization that if indeed I did enter the service and was lucky enough to not go to Viet Nam, that perhaps the whole army thing would finally make a responsible adult out of me. Perhaps if I did go into the service, I would find a skill or trade while I was in, which in turn would eventually translate into something viable, upon my return. Perhaps I then too would finally come to my senses, go back to college utilizing my veterans' benefits, and finally start taking life seriously.

That was Mom, and that was how she thought. She had this innate ability to think out both ends of everything.

My father, on the other hand, having had two hitches in the army, was far more pragmatic about the whole thing, and was fairly convinced that they wouldn't take me. *"Jesus Christ, you're a hundred pounds soaking wet, the goddamn backpack weighs more than you."*

Those words were more profound than one could imagine. Minimum weight for induction at my height of just under 5'6" was 109 pounds. The first physical that I was called for had me come in at a mere 104 pounds, and by the second physical six months later, since I had 30 days notice prior to reporting, I purposely brought myself down to just under 100 pounds with a strict diet of Jell-O, water, plain wheat crackers, and not much else. Mom's pasta and home cooking was just going to have to wait until all this bullshit was over with.

With each physical that I failed for being underweight, I then received a 1Y temporary deferment. Ultimately, after it was determined that a third physical would not be necessary, I was given the much coveted 4F permanent deferment, which then completely exonerated me from military service.

I remember finishing up that last physical, and can clearly recall the tall Black staff sergeant who manned the height and weight medical station. He apparently emanated from somewhere in the South. As he finished taking my weight and asked me to step off of the electronic scale, he said to me, *"Boy, y'all better go downstairs and get somethin' ta eat before y'all fade away, or the goddamn wind gonna take ya'll up in da air."* With that, my nightmare was over. I eventually gained back an ample amount of weight, and to some degree, I also became a bit muscular, even though I was still slim.

Some weeks later, after I received my 4F deferment card and official notice of ineligibility in the mail, I didn't hesitate to show it off to my friends like a badge of honor, while some of them were still sweating things out and waiting for their own dreaded letter telling them to report to the induction center up in Wilkes-Barre.

My gang was lucky...not one of them ended up going into the army, by virtue of having either a high number in the draft lottery, or for having some sort of physical malady that was enough to make them ineligible as well.

I absolutely hated all of the jobs that I had, and remember them all quite well.

The only thing that kept me going was a bi-weekly Friday paycheck, and knowing that in a few short hours after coming home from work, I would, almost by magic, transform into an entirely different persona, once I was out at the bar or nightclub.

It was almost like being Batman, but instead of being *Bruce Wayne by day, rogue vigilante by night*, I transformed from being *sweaty plant worker by day,* and into *well-dressed club stud by night*; but Christ, what a life it was otherwise.

The jobs *sucked*, and were typical of that which you relegate yourself to if you had at some point made a conscientious decision to do plant work your whole fucking life. You could only hope and pray that you didn't get so wrapped up in that lifestyle that you lost your life's ambition and dreams; that you didn't end up saying, *fuck it...I guess this is it for me.*

I was an order runner in a fabric dye plant, the fumes and steam of which just about killed me, and after that there was my third shift job (*graveyard shift, as they called it*) on the packing and box line in a plastics manufacturing plant, where the temperature got up to over 100 degrees inside in the summer. That job was the worst. It was pure slave labor, and on top of it all, there was not one fucking soul that I could have an intelligent conversation with, or relate to in any way.

I didn't watch football, I didn't hunt, and I wasn't into muscle cars. While they talked about *hemi car engines, deer camp, The Philadelphia Eagles, and the hot blonde from the office* at the break room table, I was somewhere else mentally. It was kind of like what you hear or read about regarding the guys who are 'lifers" in prison, and who are in solitary confinement...supposedly the only way they could keep their sanity is to simply put themselves somewhere else mentally, and that's what it might as well have been for me....*prison.*

When I look back on it now, life then was very much like being Bill Murray's character in the movie *Groundhog Day*...the nightmare repetition, the *knowing* of everything that lies ahead for the next day, and every day after that, the same conversations with the same lame-ass people *every fucking day at break time*, as well as out on the plant floor. *They talked*, and before they even got the first few words out of their mouths, I finished the sentence in my head.

Fuck me, I am getting the hell out of here, come hell or high water, I am not meant for this.

My mother was sympathetic to my plight and had a bit of clout by virtue of my politically prominent grandfather. Although he had passed away in 1967, he had bequeathed us with a family name that still bore power by virtue of *legacy* in the area and thus *favors* that could be collected on at some point in the future.

That was how politics in the area worked. You collected favors either immediately upon having done a turn for someone, or, you collected them later. In my mother's case, she was a master at collecting them later, almost as if she had them stored in a *favor bank account*.

Mom loved self-made people. She relished it, and had one conversation in particular that she used to repeat, of an individual, whose mother scrubbed floors to pay for his going to college and medical school, and who had come up from poverty to then become a physician of local prominence.

She was also a great believer in *"it's not what you know, it's who you know"*, hence, it was not beyond her to pick up the phone and use her trump card of *family name* and *favors owed* for the greater good of her son, or anyone else in the immediate family, should circumstances demand it.

In many ways, it was an *Italian thing*, and at that time in Pottsville Pennsylvania, being Italian and being connected to the right people because of family name, or, past and present affiliations, could be a game changer in terms of career path and future quality of life.

With one phone call, she had gotten me out of *box line hell* and instantly got me a job at the local water authority as a *line maintenance technician*. Translation: *I was a fucking ditch digger.*

The money was good for the day. It was a union job, there were employee benefits, and I was usually home by 5 P.M. There would be no more of my having to do *graveyard shift* in a hot smelly plant.

She was thrilled with her accomplishment. She had done her job. She had done what all mothers do...she took care of her own.

Me? I hated it. Perhaps not as much as I hated some of the sweatbox industrial plants that I had worked in, but enough to still keep me yearning, scheming, and dreaming of doing whatever it took to get the good life that I knew was somehow, some way, waiting for me. I was convinced of it.

Almost a year went by. It was now 1974, and even though I was gainfully employed with a job that paid fairly well, but which I wasn't crazy about, my prospects for anything above and beyond that didn't appear to be getting any better.

Socially I was doing great, had a somewhat steady girlfriend, a cute little thing by the name of Valerie, and was getting laid on a steady basis; if not by her, then by any number of one night stands that willingly made themselves available to me at the local night clubs or bars on my nights out with the boys.

Of course, now that I had a steady girlfriend, I absolutely had to use a condom with any other girl that I was with, if I indulged myself and snuck around on Valerie behind her back. God forbid that I would infect her because of a meaningless one-night stand; that would have been a major shit-storm.

When I look back on it now, it was really then that my lack of not being able to be faithful in a relationship truly started. I simply couldn't help myself.

It was the hunt, the chase, the magic of being with someone new, as well as the conquest and danger of it all; seeing someone you had never been with before naked for the first time, and the anticipation that precedes it; feeling them, being inside them, pleasing them; having them tell you *how good you are at fucking them.*

At the same time, it was in many ways, an escape…you're having sex, and for the next half hour or so…maybe for the whole night…all the bullshit in the world simply fades away; all the problems, all the job troubles, and the only thing that matters is that you're with *her*. There is nothing else. You simply lose yourself in the whole thing, and not even a nuclear bomb going off could distract you. It was like being in heaven.

I was addicted to pussy; it might as well have been heroin. You felt like a wizard, *a rainmaker*…and in many ways, it made up for that which was otherwise lacking in a humdrum blue-collar life in a small coal-mining town that you could easily get stuck in for the rest of your life.

Be that as it may, I remained a *dream chaser*, even though things were still not exactly looking up in any regard that would give me a new start and potentially a new life. What I did not realize was that fate was about to intervene.

Walking into work one day, I found that myself and four other people were getting job furloughed…pink-slipped, if you will. That, in turn, made me eligible to go down to what was *then called* the Federal Unemployment Office and sign up to collect a weekly unemployment check.

I did that on the same day that I was let go, driving downtown to the office, *Fog Hat* blaring full blast out of the speakers of my MG convertible…a vengeful reaction to getting screwed over by *'the man'* and having lost my job, while thinking to myself *now I'm fucked*…so much for Mom's political connections.

After having arrived and standing in line for well over an hour to sign some preliminary paperwork, I was assigned to an employment counselor to start the rigorous process of a job hunt based on my skills, or lack of, as the case may be.

I could remember sitting at his desk opposite him and looking at this guy…fat, balding, gruff voice, and an ashtray filled to the hilt with dead cigarette butts. In my mind, I could only think to myself, *what the fuck is this pathetic son of a bitch of a paper pusher going to do for me?*

He didn't appear to be any happier at that desk doing what he did, than I was, working at any of the shit-hole plant or labor jobs that I had previously.

I fantasized him saying to me, "*So, what do you like to do?*" perhaps as a half-hearted attempt to somehow find a happy niche for me, and my imaginary response in turn being "*I like to fuck and smoke weed asshole, now can you find me something where I could do that all day, you dumb shit?*" Boy was I wrong.

Looking up from his black horn-rimmed glasses, he said to me "Well, you do qualify for retraining for the workforce."

I looked at him like he had two heads, but with that, a little bell went off in my own head…

Now wait a minute, retraining equals better job, a better job equals more money, more money equals better life...and a better life equals maybe I'll get the fuck out of this town; and hey, somewhere along the line, more pussy too. Case closed.

I then asked him about what type of training was available, in which case he then began to tell me all about the *Federal Manpower Training Program*, which was the federal job-retraining program that existed then in the 70s, and which no longer exists today. He explained to me that I could retrain for any number of job areas...culinary, plumbing, electrical work, welding, etc.

That being said, let me tell you that I was not exactly jumping out of my chair at any of those suggestions, especially in light of the fact that I had just gotten out of *blue-collar hell*. The only possible exception would have been that of culinary.

Hey, after all, I *was* Italian and we *lived* for food. I had already been tutored quite well by both my mother and father in how to prepare most of the pasta and meat dishes that we ate on a weekly basis. It comes with the turf when you grow up in an Italian family. You don't just eat the food, you learn how to make it; you immerse yourself in it. It was a mandatory part of growing up Italian and of life itself, so I was definitely considering culinary...not a bad gig, provided you don't end up slinging hash in some low end local diner. Maybe, if you had the talent for it, you could actually become an upscale chef in a high-end restaurant. These were pretty much the pre-cable television years. The era of celebrity chefs such as Anthony Bourdain and Emeril that we hear about and know of today certainly did not exist then. At the time, Hollywood didn't exactly come banging down your doors because you made great pasta and meatballs. This was Pottsville....*everyone made great pasta and meatballs.*

At that point, he said the magic words..."*So, what about beauty or barber school?"*

Bingo. It was as if I was hit with lightning. As circumstances would have it, there was indeed a bit of a backstory to that little epiphany. Enter Warren Beatty, and the movie *Shampoo*.

My girlfriend Valerie and I had seen it a few weeks previous. When the movie came out, it was not only a hit; it changed the way America looked at the beauty industry.

Previous to the movie coming out, the stereotypical image of the average *male* hairdresser was that of *uber gay*, flamboyantly dressed *whackjob*, who prissed and pranced all day long in the salon, teasing comb in hand, eagerly sharing gossip with a middle-aged female clientele who relished having the companionship of what in essence was the male equivalent of a *girlfriend*, who could also be invited to dinner occasionally, and who would provide a few laughs and great conversation...*plus*...be a companion to go shopping with, and thus avail unadulterated and flareful wardrobe advice.

In retrospect, the era of modern London based *fashion hair* as well as its relationship to fashion overall, had actually already started 10 years earlier in the 60s, as part of the whole British invasion of music, Carnaby Street fashion, and Vidal Sassoon...the combined elements of which steamrollered their way across the pond to here in the United States.

From approximately 1964, and through the mid-70s and beyond, the beauty business changed radically. A new respect came for it, as well as a major change to its overall persona. There was suddenly an inclusion into its workforce, many normal heterosexual males who had a healthy love for females and a libido to match. Without question, the movie contributed in a major way to the public's awareness of those changes and was the inspiration for legions of young men to enter the field.

It was suddenly *ok* to be a male hair stylist. After the movie came out, you didn't necessarily have to worry about being labeled *a fag*, the derogatory term of the day used to describe homosexual males, as well as the presumption that *every male hair stylist was gay*. There was now a new mindset; that of male hairstylist as perhaps being that of conquering stud.

Looking back on things from my perspective today, I was at that time very homophobic, mainly because of my Italian, Roman Catholic upbringing in a small town. Thankfully, over the course of my eventual 40 plus years in the industry, it was something that I left far behind.

After having seen the movie, although I was a bit smitten with Beatty's lifestyle as portrayed in the film, I never really gave any thought to doing hair as a possible career.

Beatty, as the somewhat innocently nefarious and sexually driven character of *'George'*, the good-looking L.A. hair stylist, was getting laid right and left. His turf was Beverly Hills. He rode a motorcycle, had his blow dryer tucked in his pants, and catered to a host of Hollywood beauties and trophy wives who demanded his service in more ways than one.

It was not until seeing the movie, coupled with my fateful meeting at the unemployment office, and the counselor's subsequent mention of training for the field, that it hit me like a ton of bricks.

That day, by an act of fate, I ended up handing in my pick and shovel for beauty school, and what I optimistically perceived to be a one-way ticket to the same glamorous lifestyle that Beatty had in the movie…I jumped at the opportunity, and I didn't look back.

There was suddenly *light at the end of the tunnel*, and my entire life and future was about to change.

Chapter Three
1974 / "The Perfect Girl"

By the early summer of 1974, I was more than midway through beauty school. Without a doubt, I had made the right choice, and it opened up a whole new world for me. As well, the Manpower program paid a bi-weekly stipend plus expenses, and relieved me of having to find yet another dismal plant job in order to sustain myself while attending school.

I really loved doing hair, and surprisingly, it came naturally to me as well. I had an eye and a feeling for it. I had finally found something that I was not just good at doing, but actually, *great* at doing.

The stipend that the program paid was a then whopping $140 bi-weekly allowance for the duration of schooling, in addition to a gas reimbursement for travel back and forth to beauty school, which was in Wilkes Barre. I was still living at home with my parents, and was now finally optimistic about where I was going and what I was doing.

Pottsville had a large new enclosed mall, a first for the area, as those who lived there had previously been relegated to either going to its meager downtown area to shop, or trekking up to Wilkes-Barre to the large mall there, which had already been in place for several years.

I took a part-time job several days per week at the new mall in a store which specialized in very hip young men's clothing.

My entire persona was once again changing, and in every sense, I was now coming into my own.

Valerie and I had broken up. What was once a highly defined science of sneaking around on her on the nights that we didn't see each other, was now a new freedom of simply going out and doing as I pleased, when I pleased, and with whom I pleased…indulging myself in as many lustful nights as I wanted to up at *The Warm Up Lounge*, a well-known area night club that was about 20 minutes away, just up Interstate 81 North in Hazleton. By 1974, the popular nightclub had made the transformation from being a club that only had live rock bands, into becoming a full-blown New York style disco, with lighted dance floor and DJ. I had no one to answer to, and I liked it that way.

Because of working at the store in the mall, I had a killer wardrobe, and with the Manpower allowance I received plus my pay from the mall, I had tons of money in my pocket, *or so I perceived at the time.* I addition, I had bragging rights as to all that I was doing, and where I was headed in the future.

Life was good, and before the end of the summer was about to get even better; specifically in regards to *sex,* and in a manner which I could not possibly have fathomed beforehand. It was the summer that I met *Diana.*

My best friend Mike was dating a gorgeous blonde girl by the name of Mara, from one of the neighboring towns.

Late one afternoon, after I came home from my job at the mall, and was just settling in for a good supper, the phone rang. It was Mike. *"Get dressed and be ready for 7, we're double dating and going to the movies."* Quite taken back, I questioned his motives. *"Whoa, hold on there pal, this isn't gonna be one of your hand-me-downs now, is it?"* With a bit of a mischievous snicker, he simply said, *"Just get your ass ready, because you may well end up kissing mine after this one, buddy. Mara has a girlfriend, Diana, and trust me, you don't want to pass this one up."* With that, it was a done deal. I was in, and, I was excited.

I hurriedly finished supper, ran upstairs to shower, throw on a shit load of cologne, and change into my best outfit.

I had a pair of burgundy crushed velvet bell-bottoms as per the style of the day, as well as a white satiny semi-see-through shirt which I donned for the night. That combination was usually my *go-to outfit* when a night of special circumstances demanded it, and I absolutely had to impress. This sounded like it was *definitely* one of those nights, at least based on what Mike was telling me.

Although Mike had at times in the past coerced me into double dating with him, and me then ending up getting stuck with a girl of only barely modest looks and annoying personality, I had a premonition that this one, Diana, might possibly be someone special…someone that just might knock my socks off, and maybe even give me lurid memories of, 30 years down the road. After all, she was Mara's girlfriend, and Mara herself was as hot as a pistol. Common sense dictated that there was no fucking way that Mara was going to hang around with someone of even mediocre looks.

In my mind, the laws of the universe mandated it. Somehow, there had to be an Einsteinian equation that specifically dictated that really good-looking girls only hung out with....*other good-looking girls*, therefore making this one a no-brainer.

Mike and I had agreed to meet at his house and then take both of our cars that night. We would then meet the girls at the theatre.

Now understand the motive and the logic here: *(A) we were going to the movies, then (B) we were probably going for something to eat, and then (C) there was then going to be a good chance that at some point afterward, we might possibly go our separate ways, with both of us supposedly indulging ourselves in lustful bliss.*

We were both far too old and mature to just go *parking*, which was the stuff of teen years. Even lecherous studs like us demanded some privacy.

After meeting him at his house, we drove to the new multi-screen cinema at the mall, arriving a bit early. Although he was as cool as a cucumber since he had already been dating Mara for a number of weeks, I on the other hand was a bit nervous...unusual for me given my new level of self confidence, and probably due to my simply not knowing what to expect even though I had every reason to be optimistic that it was going to be one hell of a great night.

Within 15 minutes of our getting there, the girls pulled into the parking lot in Mara's black 1970 Corvette convertible with the top down.

As Mike uttered the words *"Here they come"*, my radar kicked in, and from a distance I could see through the windshield of the approaching car, two incredible visions of female form...sunglassed, tube-topped, creamy skinned, and the wind blowing and intertwining their hair together as if it was one until they parked and came to a stop.

I will to the day that I go to my grave and my eyes are shut, never forget the vision I saw, when Diana stepped out of the passenger side of that car.

She was quite obviously just a bit taller than I was, but not by much. She had long curly auburn hair just touching the crest of her shoulders, perfect skin with a beautiful light brown tan, and she was willowy thin with great tits. A hint of nipple pushed through the elastic red tube top she had on, which nicely countered her clingy white polyester bell-bottoms. She was wearing dainty sandals, showing off the greatest pair of tiny sexy feet that I had ever seen. She was gorgeous; *She was perfect.*

You know, it's so rare that a *perfect one* comes along. It was as if God had carved her, from head to toe, with his own hands.

Almost as if to just *dare* anyone staring at her to even *presume* of a rebellious sexuality, she was wearing a beautifully sculpted silver snake arm bracelet that was about six inches in length, and which coiled enticingly around her upper left arm. It was as though she was beckoning you by having the nerve to wear it. It said who she was, and it defined her whole look. For me, it was as if this vision was walking toward me in slow motion and making time stand still, and with that, I was quietly ecstatic.

We got the introductions over with and chatted briefly, talking about how hot it was that night. As we started to walk toward the theater entrance, she almost immediately took my hand in hers with no prompting.

With my peripheral vision, I could see her coyly turning, and giving what appeared to be a smile of approval and a quick wink to Mara.

It was apparently a sign of complete acceptance of me on her part, and perhaps a sense of relief in *her* mind that, yes, it was going to be a good night, and certainly not a night from hell, where either one of us couldn't wait for it to all be over.

As the movie had let out a bit later than usual, we agreed to skip going for a bite to eat, go directly back to Mike's house for a bit of TV, and to have a few beers. Mike's father was the night manager of a garment factory and worked third shift; his mother was in Maryland visiting her sister…thus we would have the entire house to ourselves.

Since we had met them at the theater and had taken both of our cars, Mike and I followed each other back to his house with girls in tow, the convertible tops down on both of our cars, and the wind blowing in our hair. We would take the girls back for Mara's car later at the end of the night.

During our conversation in the car, Diana and I found that we both shared a common love of rock music, and talked of bands and idols, in particular, Alice Cooper as well as some of the more popular British bands of the time….Humble Pie, Deep Purple, Uriah Heep, and many more.

We shared a joint on the way which she had pulled out of her purse without so much as even asking me if I indulged or not. By the time we arrived at Mike's house 20 minutes later, we were both as giggling, giddy, and *wrecked* as could be.

Getting out of the car, she had both arms wrapped around my waist, nuzzling her head on my shoulder, giving the small of my neck teasing flicks of kisses, and telling me how good I smelled, as we walked to the front door.

Immediately upon entering the house, Mike and Mara and Diana and I went our separate ways. Mike and Mara headed upstairs to one of the bedrooms, and Diana and I went out to the carpeted and screen enclosed back porch that had long padded lounge chairs, pull-down wicker shades, and which was also sequestered by a garden with a full border of mature 8-foot high arborvitae trees, thereby virtually assuring our privacy.

In a matter of seconds, we were at each other. It could best be described as an all out, mutual, body attack on both our parts…lips locked, hands all over each other, and pants and underwear being pulled down. It was as if a choreographed ballet of primal lust had kicked in, and *that dance* could only have one outcome.

She was, in plain words, *an animal*…the way she moved underneath me as I entered her, her whimpers and moans as I pounded her with each thrust, and her physically attempting to lift me higher with her body as I was on top of her, so as to ensure that she could get me as deep inside her as possible. We simply fucked each other's brains out, and all I could think of was *thank you God, I have my "A" game on tonight.*

I had been with quite a few girls up to that point, but never anyone like Diana. If there's such a thing as a *trophy fuck,* she was it. I don't think I have to explain why all of these years later, I can remember all of the details, as if the entire thing had just happened yesterday...who wouldn't?

Looking back on it now, I guess in some ways I had met my match. Really, perhaps she was the *female equivalent of me*; perhaps she was as obsessed with *dick* as I was with *pussy*.

We dated on and off the rest of the summer. The sex was plentiful, and about as raw and carnal as it could possibly get. She was my kind of girl...educated, highly intelligent, well spoken, poised, beautiful, and she *loved*...I mean, *truly loved* to have sex. She even knew some out of the way wooded spots where we could park the car, strip off our clothes with reckless abandon, and fuck nonstop under the stars for hours at a time. Some nights I wouldn't even get home until almost 3 A.M.

I would keep a large gray blanket in the trunk of my MG just for those occasions, and more times than not, come home with my ass and back covered in large red mosquito bites and scratches.

I can remember one Sunday morning, in particular. I had awoken, and got up out of bed after one of those *exhausting* sessions of outside summer night sex with Diana. I went downstairs to the kitchen for a Sunday morning breakfast of Mom's fried meatballs and coffee. Mom always made the sauce and meatballs for Sunday dinner early, starting her cooking before 6 A.M. so that she could attend early Mass, so by the time you were up, the *pre-sauced* fried meatballs and a cup of coffee was Sunday breakfast; typical of an Italian household.

I came downstairs and was donned only in my pajama bottoms. As I was pouring a cup of coffee for myself with my back turned to my mother, she apparently noticed the red mosquito bites on my back, as well as the scratch marks from Diana's nails, thus prompting her to ask, "*What the hell happened to you?...your back looks like it went through a damn meat grinder.*"

Thinking quickly, I amazed myself at what I could come up with on the spur of the moment...especially when I didn't want my mother to find out that I was out all night in some secluded field by a lake fucking my brains out: "*Oh, a, Mike had a flat tire last night and we had to change it, so I was laying on the ground with no blanket or anything while I was helping him.*"

With a quizzical raised brow, she gave me that *I don't believe you, but I don't want to know any more* stare of hers, that only she could give. *"Just watch yourself buster...you can't bullshit me."* She let it go at that, and returned to her cooking. I didn't say another word.

Surely, she knew I wasn't changing a tire, but at the same token, she simply didn't want to know anything else either.

One thing I had to accept, much to my disappointment, was that the whole thing with Diana was *not* going to be developing into any kind of permanent relationship.

Starting with the onset of our seeing each other on a somewhat regular but none the less non-steady basis, Diana made one thing perfectly clear to me. *"I don't do the boyfriend thing."*

That became even more evident to me on a night when I had forgotten my wallet after having driven to her house to pick her up for a night out.

Heading back home to retrieve it, and upon pulling up to the house with Diana in the front seat, my father was sitting on the front porch relaxing and enjoying one of his after-dinner *Hoya De Monterrey* cigars; something he relished doing in the summertime.

"C'mon up for a minute to say hello, I won't be long." I said.
Really, I think I just wanted to show her off. She was the most gorgeous girl I had ever dated, and had I brought her up to the porch to meet Dad, undoubtedly, his jaw would have dropped open, and at some point later with an abundance of fatherly pride, he would have probably lavished great praise on me for snagging a gorgeous looking girl of that caliber.

It's probably a good thing that she *didn't* come up to the porch with me, as inevitably both my paranoia and imagination would have kicked in upon my running into the house, and then going upstairs to retrieve my wallet. In my head, I would have *imagined* Dad being pleasantly conversational, but nonetheless giving her the third degree during my minute or two of absence...*"So, where are you guys headed tonight?"* and her simply responding *"Oh nowhere, I'm just going to fuck your son silly, that's all."*

The non-paranoid non-imaginative *reality of it* was quite different. Upon pulling up to the house and asking her if she wanted to come up to the porch for a minute while I ran in the house to get my wallet, she said *"Absolutely not"* and gave me back a rather terse looking kind of *what the fuck* stare.

Politely, she just gave my father a wave from the front seat of the car, and simply said *"Hi, nice to meet you."* Squirming a bit, she then pushed herself down and back into the passenger seat as she pulled her sunglasses back down on her face, and threw her body back into a deep reclining position. She was quite obviously as uncomfortable as could be at the thought of even getting remotely close to, let alone meeting, a parent. It just wasn't her thing.

At the end of almost every date night, and upon my asking her when she was free again in the upcoming days or week, she would actually pull out a small calendar from her purse on which she had an approximate 2-week schedule of dates with other guys in addition to the usual personal appointments and things to do.

In hindsight, I must have been, as we say in Italian, *"stunade."* Seriously, was I to expect anything less with a girl like this? Indeed, I must have been either stupid or crazy.

She always made room to see me, but my waiting on average a week before being with her again was enough to drive one mad. All I could think about for that entire week was fucking her...*again*.

If I was lucky, and circumstances prevailed, maybe I saw her two times in one week; that in itself was like an act of God.

In the big picture of things, I guess that I wanted to have my cake and eat it too. I wanted her to be my girlfriend...a sexual animal that I would have all to myself....for me to be the only one fucking her, and the bottom line with that, was simply, *with some girls, you just can't have it that way.*

By the end of the summer, Diana was getting ready to head back to begin her last year of college. Her campus was in the middle of the state almost two hours away, and she would only be coming home for the holiday breaks in November and December.

I never saw her again after our last time together in mid-August, right before she left for her senior year. As years passed, I wondered where fate had taken her.

Ironically, a few years later, when I was cutting hair down in the Philadelphia area, I ended up by mere happenstance to be doing the hair of a young lady who turned out to be her sister-in-law. The coincidence absolutely floored me.

Having married Diana's brother, she of course, bore the same last name, prompting me to ask if she had any relatives in the Pottsville area, and thus discovering the relationship.

I asked about Diana, only to find out that after college she headed to New York, and eventually worked her way up to becoming the Vice President of Operations for a major international marketing firm based out of Manhattan.

I told her sister-in-law to mention to her that I was asking about her the next time she would happen to see her, and of course, to tell her where I was now, and what I was doing.

About six or seven weeks later when she came back in for a trim, she told me that she had seen Diana a few weeks earlier. She and her husband had been home for the weekend, and Diana was home from Manhattan visiting her mother. She then said to me, *"Diana said I'm supposed to give you a big fat hug and kiss for her, and to give you her best."*

By early Fall I had finished beauty school and was eager to begin my new career. I had left my part-time job at the clothing boutique in the mall and was actually working at two different salons locally. A distant cousin of mine owned a salon in downtown Pottsville. I began as a shampoo assistant, and I was also working a few days a week at a local barbershop where I was actually allowed to take clients, and begin developing my skills doing men's hair.

I was starting to become totally immersed in the business and was more than gratified to have a viable trade...one that was both artistic and had the potential to give me a great income and a better life. Still, there was a part of me inside that kept pushing for more.

A little voice inside me told me to be leery of being trapped in a small town, in a small corner salon, and in some way end up in the same boring fucking routine that I was locked in before.

I had the ambition and knew what I wanted to achieve, but being new to the industry and having only minimal experience up to that point in time, the path out of Pottsville was nothing less than a pipe dream, and possibly a tenuous one at best.

As an avid reader of several salon industry trade periodicals that came out monthly, I idolized and followed the handful of nationally and internationally known stylists whose work and photo editorials were the subject matter inside.

Although to the average layperson outside of the business they were generally unknown, they were literally of movie star status in the industry, and had developed a legion of followers which they had cultivated around the world in the salon trade.

They were the subject of everything from salon coffee table books to product-related salon wall posters that glorified their endorsements.

They were the Gods that ruled, and in my mind at that time, were beyond my reach in any way, shape, or form.

The thought of *meeting* them was one thing, but the thought of my ever *working* in that high-end arena, or with anyone of that same caliber and nationally known status in the industry, was simply beyond my comprehension. Little did I know how fate would intervene in just a few short years.

That fall I attended my first large beauty industry trade show. One of the major beauty brands, in conjunction with a well known Northeastern Pa. based salon supply distributorship, was bringing in Paul English, the hottest guy in the business, who at that time was touring with the *Paul English Traveling Road Show*.

I can remember walking down the main hallway that led to the Grand Ballroom of the resort. I was awestruck, just seeing the oversized black and silver metal road cases on wheels that were lined up against the wall, and which were clearly stenciled in black diagonal lettering *'Paul English'*.

My God, this was more than hair; this was Rock And Roll. As my co-workers and I watched him from the fifth row up front, I was mesmerized by what he was doing.

He was brash, cocky, and wielded his scissors on several different models with both lightning speed and a degree of precision which I could have only dreamed of duplicating, as a then young novice in the business.

It was cutting edge work for the time...geometric bobs done in just six mega-sized sections, long shaggy layers that gave volume to the hair, as well as *spoke volumes* about, and personified that period of time in which we lived. It was indeed Rock And Roll, but it was far more than that...it was an eccentric genius up on stage who knew *exactly* what he was doing, *exactly* what the crowd wanted, and without question knew that he was giving an entire industry a new direction to aim for.

That show changed everything for me. I suddenly knew what I wanted to do in the industry; *I wanted to be a platform artist.* I wanted to teach, stand in front of a crowd, and hopefully getting accolades for that I which I did. I just had to figure out a path to get there.

While working at the downtown salon that I was assisting in, I met the girl who was to end up being my first wife, Maria. She was 19 and I was 24. I still, to this day, don't know what came over me; some kind of *fucked up* change in my head. Maybe it was the fact that I had so much goddamn sex with Diana that past summer and was totally burnt out, but for the first time in my life I was leaving my sexual proclivity behind, and suddenly found myself in a whirlwind courtship with this sweet, naïve young thing, who was as cute as a button, and as innocent as newly fallen snow.

In being in that relationship with her that came about, for the first time in my adult dating life, I actually found myself being faithful to someone. We got married less than a year later.

Perhaps getting married so quickly was just my consistent need to get laid on a steady basis, or maybe this whole thing was *Freudian* in some way. Maybe, in addition to being able to have sex on a continual basis, I also *thought* I was in love; I don't know. I was crazy about her...but in time, that was all going to change.

Chapter Four
1975 / The Move

By the autumn of 1975, Maria and I had the opportunity to move to the King of Prussia, Pa. area, but that occurrence was not an immediate thing.

The move out of Pottsville and down to the posh suburbs of Philadelphia was not an instantaneous act of destiny. It was actually a series of steps, all of which came about by mere happenstance and a little bit of luck. Argumentatively, the fact that I had a *big set of balls*, and was brought up to take advantage of circumstances, should they arise, certainly expedited things.

Maria and I had married just a few months previous…a small quick affair, with just our families present. After the both of us had mutually put in our licks doing hair in the Pottsville area, we were hired by a prominent national salon chain based out of California. One of my former instructors from the beauty school that I attended had a connection with the company, and acted as a consultant for their student affairs and school division. He had been contacted by their national corporate headquarters, as they were looking for viable job candidates for their new locations. He recommended me, since in his mind, I was by virtue of skill level, light years ahead of many of my peers with whom I had attended school.

The company contacted me, and both Maria and I ended up interviewing at one of their New Jersey locations, getting hired, and accepting staff positions at the company's Lancaster, Pa. location which was within one of the larger malls located on Route 30 just outside of the city. The move was something which neither Maria nor I was crazy about, but accepted anyway, given that we were both so anxious to get out of Pottsville and finally strike out on our own.

At the time, there were no staff openings in any of the chain's Philadelphia area salon locations, so getting our foot in the door one way or another was the thing to do.

After putting in roughly a year in Lancaster, that opportunity to transfer to King of Prussia to what was then going to be the company's largest and most modern salon came about quite by accident.

The mid and late 70s was, of course, the *golden era* of malls. Their existence gave the opportunity for many well known salons to develop multiple locations, and then further develop themselves to a next level and become a nationally recognized brand.

In the process, they would then be in an enclosed shopping environment that promised the potential of high traffic and high service dollar volumes. This would then become an opportunity to work with retail developers on a repeated basis and become *huge* nationwide, potentially having hundreds of mall-based salons, and employing thousands of stylists, while gaining national notoriety for both their mall presence and persona as a brand.

I jumped at the chance for us to transfer to King of Prussia from Lancaster. I had been down to Philadelphia and its outlying suburban area numerous times before, in my late teens and early twenties for concerts, and to partake in its abundant nightlife, which consisted of super hip nightclubs, great eateries, and to go shopping for the latest trend clothing at the area's wide assortment of high fashion stores.

I got to know the area quite well. King of Prussia had a fashion savvy demeanor that was far ahead of anything that Pottsville had to offer, and for that matter, anywhere else in Northeastern Pa., in general…but there were other reasons too.

That area had long been resplendent in upscale New York style hair salons, and from the early beginning of my career prior to moving there, I was made well aware of it.

When I was still cutting hair in Pottsville, I could remember a number of occasions when I would get the occasional *pain in the ass* and supposedly *uber hip* female client in my chair. They would regale me with tales of girlfriends or acquaintances that had made the hour and a half trek down to either Philadelphia proper, or its suburbs, to get their hair cut by the so-called masters of the hair scene down there.

To listen to these tales of *super chic* salons that embellished their clients with wine and did cutting edge work infuriated me. I was a struggling young upstart trying to convince anyone who sat in my salon chair in Pottsville that I *knew what the fuck I was doing,* and that I was fairly good at it; at that time, maybe not an expert, but reasonably good, given the fact that I was only in the business a year or so.

As such, all I simply wanted from anyone who sat in my chair in the salon was a little goddamned respect.

What the fuck...you're in my chair now, and you obviously came here for a reason, so why are you telling me about all of these other fucking salons, and why aren't you down there in the 'land of the hair gods' letting one of them cut your hair, if they're so fucking good? I didn't *say it*, but I sure as hell *thought it*.

For me, at that time, because I was still living and working in such a small town such as Pottsville was, the possibility of working in Philadelphia, or its surrounding area, was the *gold standard* of everything that I wanted to do and accomplish in the beauty industry. The only exception to that would be my somehow being lucky enough to end up in L.A., or perhaps in New York. If indeed I was going to stay in Pennsylvania, and make something out of myself in the business, then Philadelphia or the surrounding area would be the place to be at.

As it turned out, getting transferred there from Lancaster was as simple as being within earshot of a conversation that I accidently overheard going on between a company Vice President, who was visiting the Lancaster salon for the day, and Jerry, the salon manager, as they discussed plans on future company expansion.

I happened to overhear *King of Prussia* being mentioned, and my ears perked up faster than a dog in heat.

I simply intervened on my own behalf, and told Frank, the visiting VP, how much I loved that area. During the conversation, I verbally demonstrated to him a working knowledge of both the dynamics and demographics of the area. It couldn't have been easier.

He was so impressed, he almost immediately offered me an option for both myself and Maria to transfer to King of Prussia.

A major expansion and renovation of one of the larger malls was underway and our new state of the art salon would be in a primary corridor that was being added on with the expansion.

Maria and I would go as a husband and wife team, enhanced by the fact that there were two other couples, one married and one not, who would also be part of the opening staff there as well.

In a matter of months, as the new addition to the mall neared its opening date, we were en-route down to the Philadelphia area via an all expense paid company move, as well as the promise of a far more resplendent life than was offered in Lancaster at the time.

What I didn't realize was how that move, as well as the affiliation with the L.A. based salon chain, would end up with my having the most formative years of my career, and that it would also be the conduit to my finally being able to *play with the big boys* in the industry. What I *also* didn't realize, or should I say, what I really hadn't given any thought to at that time given my supposed *marital bliss*, was that working in a large high-end metropolitan mall such as that would be, was to put it simply, *like working in pussy heaven*.

The mall that we worked at in Lancaster was also a very large mall, however, in 1975 Lancaster was nowhere near being the diverse melting pot or upscale cosmopolitan retail mecca that King of Prussia was; nor did it offer the potential lifestyle that King of Prussia did. It was, at that time, about as boring of an area that you could possibly live in, with very little nightlife or city-like ambiance and persona.

Walking down the long mall corridors, what you saw were large gatherings of Amish and Mennonites, simple blue-collar shoppers, and tons of people whom you knew from first sight, were farmers.

Lancaster simply bored the living hell out of me, and if I had been asked one more time *"Ohhh, so you're I-talian?"* (the emphasis being on the 'I'), I was going to deck the shit out of someone. All I could then think to myself was *Christ, what a bunch of fucking hicks...get me the hell out of here.*

Aside from the mall, Lancaster's primary notoriety was not just for its large Amish population, but also for the seemingly endless miles of sprawling green farmland. On the busy causeways just off of Route 30 that offered shopping and restaurants, it was not unusual to see horse-drawn carriages and tourists gawking at the sight of young Amish boys in straw hats, men with long beards, and women wearing white bonnets. The women would cover themselves with long sleeved purple or black dresses, depending on their sect, that were well below the knee. Even in the extreme heat of July or August, *suffering* seemed to be an intrinsic part of Amish life.

Maria and I were living in a beautiful modern apartment complex just off of Route 30. Because Lancaster had an abundance of fertile farmland, many times we had to shut our windows during the summer, because of the foul fragrance of horse manure that was used to fertilize the farm fields that were adjacent to our apartment building. Thank God, we had central air conditioning, and didn't have to open the windows all of the time.

I really hated the whole Pennsylvania Dutch thing. Everywhere you looked, there was a billboard or large sign for either a tourist stop, a restaurant, or a Dutch-themed store, and it seemed as though *they all used that same fucking logo*...usually an oversized, twenty foot tall figure of a Pennsylvania Dutchman in wide-brimmed dark hat, long beard, corn cob pipe in mouth, and a wink in his eye, saying some catchy Germanic accented phrase like 'Yahhhhhh, Get to know vat goooooood is'. It was a script to beckon in the many tourists with tons of money to spend.

I couldn't stand it. I was thrilled to be out of Pottsville, *but this shit*; this was certainly not what I was looking for.

We made the move to King of Prussia in August of 1975, just a few weeks before the early September grand opening of the new mall addition.

Our first year was hectic, and a bit crazy. The mall was jammed most of the time, as was our salon. Although we operated primarily by appointment, the premise of a so-called *family hair salon* located in a major mall, and offering the ability to just walk in for a haircut, or make an appointment for services, was generally new.

The competition was tough. There were four other national salon chains within the mall, and each of the major anchor stores had salons within, as well.

In a relatively short time, we had a staff of about 18 stylists, the majority of them working full time to keep up with the demand. In addition, the training on the technical methods of all of the newest hair trends was demanding and intense, and it led to our being one of the best-trained salon staffs in the entire area.

Because the salon was fast becoming the new *golden goose* of the entire chain via the service volume we did, we were in many ways catered to regarding our training. Much of it was done personally by the company Director of Training, Frederick Bacherman, who was a world-class haircutter and stylist in his own right.

The training was usually done after work, starting at 9 P.M., with sessions sometimes lasting well past midnight. It was then followed by our having to be back at the salon the next morning for 9 A.M. for the start of a new day. It was exhausting, but well worth it.

The company was well aware of our ever-growing stellar status in the area and took nothing to chance, providing an extensive marketing program involving both print and electronic media. We were pumping out numbers that made corporate management in California take notice and send us letters of accolade. On more than one occasion, the local newspaper ran articles touting our success as one of the top salons in the area.

From a personal growth standpoint, my skills were becoming top notch, as well.

Beyond the fact that I had a natural aptitude and ability for cutting hair, I simply devoured every bit of training that was thrown at me, and in our business you either *get it* or *you don't*. In my case, I not only *got it*, but also milked it for all it was worth.

I absolutely *loved to cut hair*; in fact, I lived for it. I did a bit of hair color too, but really, my personal forte' was to have scissors in hand…flailing away with my newfound artistic madness and creativity.

It didn't take long for me to become booked solid with clients by appointment several weeks in advance, and throughout the salon, mall, and the immediate suburban King of Prussia area I was very quickly making a reputation for myself as being *the 'go to guy'* for a great haircut.

I had made it. Life was good. I finally lived in a great city, and was doing that which apparently my destiny called for.

Back home, word of both my move *and* my stellar ability with shears traveled fast. I soon had quite a few people from Pottsville, as well as the surrounding area, coming down to King of Prussia to get their hair cut by me.

Now *I was the guy* who people traveled almost an hour and a half to see; *I was the guy* that the would-be fashionistas back home were talking about, and the karma of it all was sweet indeed.

The mall, being a mecca of high-fashion clothing stores, as all modern malls were, was loaded with tons of great looking young women who were either working part-time at one of the many high-end clothing stores while making their way through college, or in some cases looking to make a long term career out of retail; perhaps hoping to eventually become a manager, district manager, or maybe even become a buyer.

The list of iconic brand stores that were in the mall from that time in the 70s was endless, as was the bevy of gorgeous young things who worked in the mall and became my steady clients.

It was actually quite stressful for me to handle in many ways, as my past penchant for women was beginning to overtake the almost two years that I had clearly devoted to being faithfully married…a marriage which itself too, was finally starting to get stressful and boring. I could feel myself drifting back to my old ways on an almost daily basis.

When any one of them would sit in my chair, I always had my *A-game* on, knew how to subtly flirt, give them my pose, walk the walk, and talk the talk.

I was on autopilot, and it came naturally, but I had to constantly be vigilant of my wife Maria, who worked 4 chairs down from me, and of her then overhearing my conversations. Eventually, when we were at home, she would at times relentlessly bust my balls and read me the riot act for what she perceived to be that of my being *on the make*; but at the same token, so were *they*, the women that sat in my chair. It was obvious that many of them could give a shit less if you were married, by virtue of their comments and aggressive flirting.

It was maddening. You get these girls in your chair, and at times it was almost overwhelming; they just looked so damn good, smelled so damn good, were dressed provocatively, and had no qualms about being sexually aggressive in their demeanor. In addition, as part of our business, indeed, something which is very unique to our business, you get to touch them almost immediately, vis a vis touch their hair within nothing less than 5 seconds of their having sat down in the salon chair, simply because you had to do an initial consultation with them, and discuss what they wanted to have done.

Surely, I had one hell of a multitasking brain, as I had the ability to stay highly focused on the whole hair thing when a good-looking female client was in my chair, yet at the same time, be saying to myself in the back of my head, *God in heaven, what I wouldn't give to break my dick off in your ass.*

As the weeks and months went by, the social dynamic of the staff became one of closeness. We were spending roughly 10 to 12 hours a day working together, and were really starting to know each other inside out. As a result, a gang of us would many times go out at night after work to one of the many local nightclubs or watering holes.

Most of the staff was single and female, with the exception of the three couples who were married or simply living together, including Maria and I. There were a few single guys on the salon staff as well.

Those of us who were couples generally hung out together on a regular basis, but it was not unusual for all of the guys to go out by ourselves without our spouses or girlfriends, in order to blow off some steam; especially when we frequented the upscale strip clubs that were in the area.

There were a few nightclubs and bars where it seemed that the entire working population of the mall hung out after work, and on those nights that I was out, either by myself or with a few of the guys, I was able to both freely converse and flirt with those same female clients of mine who worked at the mall and *also* gave me a *raging hard-on*. I was clearly in a position to take advantage of it as well, especially when Maria was not out with me on a given night.

I had developed a local *celebrity* of sorts, loved the immediate attention I would get when I walked into a club or bar, and as I became more and more caught up in it all, I was starting to go out almost every night. For me, it was further enhancing the fact that my marriage had already started to fall apart.

I was starting to become one of the *night people,* and I loved it as much as I was beginning to *hate* being married.

I loved going out at night…the music, the excitement, and the crowd…being with *the people of the night.* It was as though we were a select group, and in many ways, we were peers. If you weren't out clubbing on a given night, inevitably, the next morning when you saw your friends at the mall coffee kiosk, they would ask where you were the previous night, and tell you how you had missed one hell of a good time.

Truly, I think that when I was in my mid twenties, I had a physical constitution made out of iron. I was able to stay out all night, drink like a fish, and not come home until 2 A.M.

Somehow, I was still able to get up at 7 A.M. in the morning, in order to be at the salon for a 9, start another 12-hour day, and in most cases, repeat the same routine at least four or five times a week. It was grueling, but it was *also* intoxicating. *It owned you*, and it simply would not let go. It was as if the whole club scene was a lethal pheromone that enveloped your senses, making you nothing short of crazy, and when you combined that environment with all of the testosterone pumping inside you, it was like rocket fuel propelling you on an endless flight. If you then put a little weed and cocaine into the mix, you were a fucking maniac that felt invincible. Truly, on those nights, I had enough balls to go up to any girl and ask her for a go, and being married at the time didn't stop me.

I was out of control, it was happening to me *again*, and I didn't miss so much as a heartbeat.

The arguments with Maria were becoming daily battles of where I was the night before, who I was with, and how she was sick and tired of staying home alone.

She, in turn, started to go out with the girls from the salon quite a bit, and the whole thing became a game of *one-upmanship.*

Sex with her, what little of it there was when we were not arguing, was becoming laborious, mechanical, and boring. I should have stayed in my niche. I should have married one of the *bad girl*s. Perhaps that would have stopped me from regressing back to the way that I was. I would have supposedly been content on all fronts.

I did the stupidest thing that a guy like me could do. I married for an attraction to innocence during a period of my life when my guard was down, *and my dick didn't rule my brain.* It turned out to be a major mistake.

Chapter Five
Demons

It happens. Just when you think that you have your life squared away because you're approaching the age of 30, married, own a house, have a viable career, and have supposedly purged all of the things from your irresponsible past, your old ways come back to haunt you.

In my case, I had a marriage that was progressively getting worse by the day, and I had a veritable smorgasbord of women available to me at the mall, so it didn't take much to push me over the edge and find the demons back in my head.

You're around women all day, *good-looking women*, and they're all over the damn mall, plus, you're doing maybe a dozen or so female clients in the salon each day, and damn, you just want to fuck them all…or at least *most* of them.

I don't care how happily you're married. If indeed, you were one horny son of a bitch during what was previously your single life, the fact of the matter is that even after you're married, happily or otherwise, or are in a long term relationship with someone, *you're still going to look, and you're still going to lust,* and when you lust, you usually do two things…you imagine any fine young thing that you see, *naked,* and you repeat that same phrase in your head that you've repeated a thousand times before: *God, I'd like to fuck the shit out of her*…but you *can't*, because you're married. That's the way it's *supposed* to be.

Christ, I couldn't even walk down the mall corridor to go to lunch, at one of the mall eateries. The fact that I got the stares, knew how to make the right eye contact, and heard the whispered comments when I passed groups of young twenty-something libertines didn't help matters, either.

It was as though I owned the place. It was like being *King of the Mall*.

As I would walk down the mall corridor, I knew everyone and they knew me. I'm not just talking about the many female acquaintances that I had made, be they clients who might be out for a day of shopping in the mall, or girls that I would recognize from my nights out in the clubs, but *especially* the working girls in the mall.

I probably could have gotten laid ten times over if there was such a thing as an all-day lunch, and I didn't have to go back to the salon.

I was lucky to cram in a sandwich and a Coke, simply because when I was headed from and back to the salon at lunchtime, I was just too busy fucking around, looking around, and flirting. Some of it was because I provoked it, and some of it was because I was simply approached. I literally had my pick, and it was starting to make me a bit crazy.

I *thought* I was over it, and was constantly trying to have a rational thought process in my head, trying to be strong, and trying to talk common sense to myself. After all, I had obligations now...*adult obligations*....house, wife, job, and building a career. For some of us, that way that we were just keeps coming back, pulling you down like a thousand pound weight chained to your legs while you hang from a fucking cliff, as it generates that which could only be described as extreme self-inflicted doubt about the life decisions that you had made. It's then that those demons come back to haunt you, and it's like a slap up the side of the head, with them saying to you, *Hey fucker, we're not through with you just yet.*

You fight it, and more times than not, you lose. The demons will have their way. It's like those little caricatures that we've all seen in a thousand TV cartoons when we were kids; *The Devil*, representing evil, is on one shoulder, hastening you with pitchfork in hand to continue on some debaucherous path, and then on the other shoulder, *The Angel* of everything good, complete with halo and wings, telling you, *don't even fucking go there asshole*, but for some reason you still do.

In 1977, I was named to the company's National Education Team. The company had been growing by leaps and bounds and Frederick, our Director of Education, was swamped traveling from salon to salon, in multiple states to train all of the staff.

The need arose for a company-wide team consisting of the *creme de la creme* of stylists from within the company to travel extensively, teach seminars, and do in-salon training on both a regional and national basis.

With my being named to the team I had carved out a place for myself in that upper echelon that I had long desired to be part of, ever since the beginning days of my career working at a local corner salon in Pottsville.

I was now part of an elite group within the company, and had elevated myself to that status in just under 36 months of being in the business.

Not bad for a poor Italian boy from *the hill,* who just a few years previous was working on a packing line in a plastics plant with a bunch of *douche bags* who only knew beer and cars…only I had escaped.

In addition to continually developing my skills cutting hair, I had also developed an expertise in everything and anything related to the formulation and use of the company's extensive in-house product line.

I was not only named to the team, but was also asked to take a formative part in the continuing creation and expansion of that line.

I was now tasked with talking to the manufacturers and chemists, giving them insight, doing field testing on the products, and reporting back to Frederick, who had moved up from being the Director of Education, to become a VP and board member, resulting in his having to move to the West Coast where the corporate offices were located.

My promotion could not have come at a worse time, given the state of my crumbling marriage as well as my then conflicted state of mind.

I was suddenly heaped with new responsibilities, but also, as was mandated by company protocol regarding the team's image, expected to be a role model.

Everyone in the salon knew that Maria and I were very near a split, but were just keeping peace with each other and bearing it out.

They all saw me out in the clubs at night. They saw me leave a bar or club numerous times, with someone on my arm, no matter how low-key I tried to keep it. They might not have said anything, but they *knew* what I was like.

It was almost laughable…me, as a supposed role model. Perhaps I might be the role model for everything hair related, but beyond that, being a role model otherwise was the last thing that I was.

Being part of that team was something that I had really wanted. I knew damn good and well that it was absolutely of prime importance that I not *fuck the whole thing up*. It was a perfect gig for me, and for that matter, for my ego. I was doing things that I never dreamed that I would be doing.

Here I was now, the company products guru, and with the blessing and encouragement of the corporate hierarchy was talking on a regular basis with many of the top chemists in the salon product arena. I was assigned to tell them how I thought formulas should be changed, discuss problems with bottling and packaging, and inform them about the latest product trends I thought we as a salon chain should start to work on.

Frankly, more times than not, it was a *pinch me, I'm dreaming* type of moment whenever I was conversing with them on the phone. The team was in many ways catered to, and as such, if we were to be out in the field training young stylists and staff, then of course by Frederick's mandate and astute oversight we on the team also had to be exposed to the very best that the industry had to offer at the time.

Our training was intense and competitive. As the team varied in size from time to time, usually averaging about 10 of us to cover all of the company salons nationally, we were also being exposed to, trained by, and rubbing elbows with, a veritable *who's who* of the salon industry. Just a few years previous, I would have only dreamed about meeting them, let alone being personally trained by them.

The company training facility was in Columbus, Ohio and we would all meet there.

My memories are vivid. One memory in particular, is the time that the entire team was having dinner with one of the legendary stylists and educators from London, who shall remain nameless. He had done a day long training session for us. At that time, he was one of the best editorial stylists in the business, and was now one of the top stylists in New York City. After dinner, we stayed up past midnight, and he regaled us with stories of his former British colleagues…all of whom we knew by name and industry reputation. He talked about living and working in swinging London during the 60s, which was then the *heyday* of British hair. We sat, elbows perched, and just listened, our mouths open and drooling.

There were others as well...master hair stylists and artistic directors from many of the top hair styling organizations and companies from across the board in the entire industry. The list of names and and notable people that we were trained by was extensive.

It was a glorious time, and for me, being otherwise preoccupied with who I could fuck, and when I could fuck them, while being in a marriage that I didn't want to be in, my being on the team as well as being in the company of such industry luminaries, was probably the only glue that held me together and saw me through. It was then that I met Rita...*lovely Rita.*

She was one incredible and sexually demanding little dynamo, packed into a slightly more than five foot tall 100-pound frame, that demanded nothing less than 1000 percent sexual performance on my part.

She was second generation Italian, somewhat dark complected, and had long, naturally curly dark hair, in addition to having *great* almond-shaped eyes that just penetrated you. She also had killer legs, always coming in for her appointments *dressed to the nines*, with high heels on to show off her great looking tan legs.

She flirted with me from the first time that she came in as a client, and made it clear that she wasn't attached, nor did she care if I was. This became a bit problematic, given her aggressive flirting when she came in for a haircut. It was to the point that it could have gotten me into *deep shit*, with my wife in such close proximity.

I had to watch my ass at all times when I was working in the salon, but here I was, cutting her hair, with my wife working just a few chairs down from me. Rita thought nothing of making open sexual innuendo during our conversation while I was cutting her hair. She would sometimes grab at my dick with her hand from under the cape when I happened to be in *just the right position* in front of her, or kick off one of her shoes and mischievously rub the side of my leg with her foot as I was doing the front lines of her long shaggy cut.

I knew this girl was looking for action from the very first time she came in. She asked me if I was married, and upon my telling her that I was, she then said, *"Wow, what a waste."* It was, without question, a clear indication of what she wanted, and what she was looking for.

We met secretly for lunch outside of the mall on several occasions, and of course, we both knew where the hell this was headed.

This girl could get you hot just by the way that she looked at you with those great eyes of hers, the way she smoked, and her entire body language. To watch her smoke a cigarette, all you could think about was that if she gave a blowjob the same way that she smoked, you were in for one hell of a treat. It was a visual thing, but it spoke volumes.

We finally got together when Maria had gone to New Jersey for the weekend to see her mother and stepfather, who owned a timeshare condo at the Jersey Shore for extended vacations. I met her at one of the local clubs one night, but knew that I had to keep our eventual departure low key, as there were at least four of my female co-workers there, all of whom had loose tongues, and were buddy-buddy with my wife. We had planned ahead of time to leave separately, but not before there was *almost* an all-out catfight between Rita and another girl that I used to bang on occasion, who worked at one of the mall clothing stores...Charlene. Charlene was half-Asian, was also quite tiny, and was quite the cute little dish herself.

Rita and I were at the bar conversing, and she excused herself to go to the restroom. Charlene came over to *make her move,* saying to me *"So are you with her or what? I thought she'd never leave."* She then looped her arm around mine, with a clear expectation level of what could happen that night.

I was in no mood, and my focus for the night was on Rita. Looking at her, I said *"Charlene...again?"* I was trying to get the point across to her that I had something else going on, and that I had no intention of ending up with her that night. She looked at me quite surprised, and with a lurid smile on her face, as if she thought she could salvage the situation. *"You didn't say that last week when your dick was in my mouth, now, did you? You enjoyed that, didn't you, you egotistical prick?"*

With that she stretched up a bit to plant a soft kiss on my cheek, teasingly bit my ear, and whispered, *"Get rid of her and I'll suck on that beautiful cock of yours tonight until you pass out."* It was tempting. Indeed, she was an expert at knowing how to please a man in that way. After a minute or so of conversation, and just as I was once again giving her that look of *this is not going to happen tonight Charlene*, I could see Rita making her way back through the crowd. It was quite obvious to me, even from ten feet away, that she was pissed off in a major way.

From the look in *those* eyes…those fantastic eyes of hers that she could use as a lethal weapon or a tool of seduction, she obviously saw Charlene with her arm provocatively entwined with mine, and was nothing short of furious. *"Fuck off, he's with me."* Charlene, throwing down the gauntlet, fired back *"What are you, his fucking keeper? Honey, let me tell you something, we're all just another good night to him, so don't think you're anything special…take a number."*

For a brief moment, I thought Rita would gouge her eyes out, and that a shoving match would then ensue. With that, I was hastily scouring the immediate area to make sure that none of my co-workers who were there saw or overheard what was going on in the event that I had to separate the both of them.

Thankfully, civility, if you could call it that, took reign. Rita, giving me that look that only she could give said, *"I'm going out to the car…either you're fucking her or you're fucking me, so make a choice and make it quick."*

As I turned to the bar to retrieve my cash and car keys, Steve who was one of the regular bartenders, and who had undoubtedly seen and heard this scenario played out countless times before on countless nights with so many others, gave me a half smile and said, *"Hey, tough choice there, pal."*

I threw a twenty on the bar, and referring to Charlene said, *"Stevie, take care of her all night, will ya?"*

Charlene, not one to be bought, bitched, or turned down, was wild with scorn. She grabbed the bill, ripped it in two, and crumpled it up, throwing it at me as I turned and walked away trying to make as quick and stealthy of an exit as I possibly could. I felt the tight paper ball hit the back of my head as it made its mark, accompanied by *"Fuck you asshole."*

Hearing that, I made a kind of stunned half turn, but I didn't look back completely…it just wasn't worth it. *Sometimes you just have to lose one to win one.*

Less than an hour later, Rita and I were in bed at my house. With Maria gone and no one home, the driveway was dead black upon our arrival. The outside lights were not on in their usual welcoming way, thus concealing from my neighbors the fact that I was bringing someone home who *wasn't* my wife.

Dick and Sandy were my neighbors who lived next door...nice people, but nosey as hell. Thankfully, they weren't out on their deck that night, and didn't see us. The only sound that we heard upon our entrance from the dark driveway into the front door of the house was that of crickets, on what was otherwise a warm peaceful summer night.

Fucking Rita was like fucking a *Stairmaster*...you worked for everything that you got, and she was not easily orgasmic, something she readily admitted to. In essence, she challenged you with that. Being as sexually open as she was, she had no qualms about telling you that very few guys were able to get her off.

As much as she loved sex, her lack of ability to get off at times clearly infuriated her. *She* tried harder, so *you* tried harder, and when she locked her legs around your waist, moving like a bucking bronco beneath you, you wondered if she would ever let go.

She *loved* to undress in front of you, and had it down to an art form...I'm not talking about cheap striptease, I'm talking about the way that she did it.

She would start to take off her clothes in the most seductive way that you could imagine, and it was as though she knew her eyes were her best weapon; they never left you as she took everything off slowly, one piece at a time from maybe ten feet away. When she was done undressing and was naked, she would slowly and seductively walk over, put one arm around my neck, and with the other, reach down to gently stroke me. As she did, she would lean up and whisper softly in my ear, *"Are you ready to fuck me? Are you ready to give me that gorgeous cock of yours, and fuck me all night?"*

She knew exactly what to say, how to say it, and when to say it, and by the time you were ready to put it inside her, you were already as hard as a brick and bursting at the seams.

She was highly experimental sexually, and was willing to do anything...*I mean, anything.* She loved pleasing men, and she verbally made you aware of what she wanted you to do. "*Fuck me harder, don't stop; God, I love your cock so much, I want you to cum inside me so bad.*" Fucking her was always incredibly physical and always intense. I swear, every time we had sex, I dropped 5 pounds, and we were both soaking wet with sweat.

I had not been put to task with anyone like that since the summer of '74 and the exhausting three months I spent dating *Diana*. Christ, this girl would get downright pissed, if she didn't have an orgasm...for her *it wasn't over until she said it was over.*

We had a clandestine affair that lasted on and off for about 3 months, and I'm sure a few people in the salon were aware of it, no matter how secretive our getting together was. I'm sure that my wife also suspected that *something* with someone was going on, but things were at a point where she just simply tolerated it, and quite frankly, I was just too adept at covering my tracks. She was constantly suspicious of me, constantly questioning me, and it didn't help matters in any way.

Even though we were living under the same roof together, it was as though the marriage didn't exist. We certainly didn't have sex anymore, we barely spoke to one another other than when necessary, and we would go our separate ways on a daily basis. There was an acceptance of the whole thing on her part, and she had apparently just acclimated herself to the way things were, and the way that I was; certainly she was not happy about it and just put up with it.

Generally speaking, she and I kept peace in the salon, and on occasion would even go out with one of the other couples that we worked with, but the fact of the matter was that it was all just a façade, and things were in all probability coming to an end, sooner than later.

As I was starting to do more company travel, doing seminars for individual salons or as part of the team, occasionally flying to the corporate headquarters on the West Coast, my affair with Rita simply ended, but slowly. The hookups became few and far between, and the simplicity of it all, as well as our being available to get together on a regular basis, just became more difficult.

Eventually, she stopped coming to me for haircuts, something which I sensed was going to happen, but at the same token, there was never an emotional attachment between us...at least not on my part. It was, from the beginning, nothing more than sex, or at least for me it was. Surely, it was nothing more than mutual gratification, self-serving to both of us.

The entire affair just stopped. It was as though we were both two sharks who had made our individual conquests in a given territory of the ocean, and now it was time to move on to other prey. Toward the end of things, she sent a note addressed to me at the salon, and which was marked *personal and confidential*. All it said was one sentence: *I miss your cock*, followed by the typical love and kisses sequence of x and o. I didn't respond. I simply had too much on my plate and I wondered if I would ever see her again.

The travel that I was doing opened up a whole new world for me. Every weekend I was in a different state, teaching at a different salon, and, had different women in my bed while I was out on the road.

My lack of control was to a point whereby I didn't even consider it a lack of control. For me, it was normal behavior that I didn't think twice about; it was the way things were, but that behavior was about to open up a whole new can of worms and almost cost me my job.

Chapter Six
Be Careful What You Wish For

By late 1979, both the salon and the company education team were firing on all eight cylinders.

As a salon, we were known as one of the top salons in the entire suburban Philadelphia area, given the amount of talent that we had within, and the dollar volume that we were pumping out on a weekly basis. The team was now tasked with training the personnel in the existing salons, as well as the new mall locations that were opening nationally at a rate of at least two per month. The company was hitting a peak. Proudly, I was part of the whole thing and playing a major role.

I absolutely loved all of the traveling that I was doing. I was 28 years old, and less than 5 years previous, I hadn't been more than 100 miles outside of the small former coal-mining town that I once called home. In terms of skill level, in just a few short years, I went from literally *not being able to cut my way out of a paper bag*, let alone do high fashion haircuts, to hopping on a plane and traveling all over the United States, teaching the latest methods of haircutting. I was also overseeing large national seminars for the company, in addition to jumping in my car to do much of the same thing on a smaller, more localized regional level in New Jersey and Southern New York, as well as at our two other Philadelphia area locations.

In due time, I had accumulated an extensive travelogue of having gone to all of the company's major metropolitan locations...Denver, Dallas, Baton Rouge, Seattle, Indianapolis, San Francisco, as well as many other cities. The level of excitement that it created for me *then* was as though someone had given me a carte blanche trip to Tahiti each week. In terms of where I was at career-wise, I was out of the Farm Leagues was now and batting in Yankee Stadium.

Out of all of the travel that I did, my great love was going to New York City.

Manhattan energized me in a way that no other city did, and I simply fell in love with it. My toes were tapping from the time I would get off of the bus at the Port Authority Terminal. I learned the city and its ways in a relatively short period of time.

As a team, most of the group would go to the International Hair Show held there each spring at what was then the premier convention facility in Manhattan, The Coliseum. The Coliseum would eventually be torn down and replaced by the Jacob Javits Civic Center, where the show is now held each year, up to present day.

Although that show is still one of the major national events in our industry, it is dwarfed by other shows across the globe. At that time though, it was *the* show of shows to attend and be seen at, and a *must go to, must be there* event.

As Vice President of Education, Frederick was always on top of his game in providing the team with advanced education from the best people in the industry. He also had many close valuable professional relationships with most of the top stylists who were the headliners of the beauty business both nationally and internationally.

Attending that show was not just an *event socialogic'* as the French would say, but an opportunity, given the connections that Frederick had, for all of us on the team to attend the private parties and lavish affairs that were usually reserved for only the top echelon of the industry.

On one occasion in particular, I believe it was the '79 show, he was able to score VIP tickets for an event called *Showcase International*, which was being held at a private conference center on 57th Street. This was an *invitation only* event, usually standing room only, and featured every major haircutter on the planet.

The venue was jammed with at least a thousand fellow artisans, and I clearly remember the sweat dripping off of me as I struggled to see the stage and its offerings from where I was, 50 feet away and down on the floor. I happened to look up to the brass-railed balcony above me, *and there he was*...Paul English, the man, the god, the guy who at that time had been completely changing our industry.

I was transfixed as I looked up at him in all his mustachioed, ascot-wearing glory. I immediately thought back to the beginning of my career, just a few years previous, and how after first seeing him cut hair on stage while attending my first professional trade show, it was he who ignited the fire in me that had not stopped burning since.

Although I was down on the floor with the rest of the team, I was not about to let the possible opportunity of my both meeting and conversing with him get by me. I told the group *"I'll be right back,"* and made my way through the crowd and up the back stairway to the balcony.

Once I got there, I slowly wiggled my way into a position almost right next to him, where he was leaning over the balcony rail.

I can distinctly remember that at the time, he was heckling one of his fellow iconic artists down on the stage who had been his former close colleague and salon-mate from the 60s when they were both coming up in the U.K., and when London and Carnaby Street ruled everything in both hair and fashion.

Webster's dictionary defines the word 'aura' as *"the highly distinctive atmosphere, emanation, or quality that seems to surround, and be generated by, a person."* As I nervously approached him and introduced myself, I swear, that is indeed what I felt and saw just being in his presence.

Upon seeing me, he then turned slowly. As he adjusted the long fashionable scarf draped around his neck, he casually threw it over his shoulder to get it out of his way, and took a heavy drag from his cigarette. His eyes pierced me as he gave me a visual top to bottom. He stumbled a bit, and with drink in hand, he had a look on his face like *Who the fuck is this guy?*

"Do I know you, mate?" Perspiring nervously, I answered him, *"No, you don't, I'm with Frederick Bacherman's crew downstairs and I just wanted to say hello and tell you how much I admired your work."*

He feigned politeness at that point. Maybe he just had too much alcohol in him. *"Oh yes, Frederick...yes indeed."*

I couldn't quite tell if he was humoring me, or just trying to be amicable for the sake of the conversation. It appeared as though he was looking at me like a fly that had to be swatted, but honestly, it didn't matter to me....*I was talking to God.*

Much to my surprise, he invited me into his little balcony circle. *"Come join us,"* he said. Perhaps he liked the fact that I had big balls, and for a few brief minutes, we chatted.

The drink that he had in his hand was definitely not his first of the evening, and probably wouldn't be his last. His appetite for booze was legendary, but then again so was his prowess as one of, if not *the most innovative* geniuses in our entire industry.

He continued to heckle his former mate that was down on stage, a cocky smile on his face, always followed by approving chuckles from his entourage of admirers and the *yes-men* that surrounded him, as well as then getting a few laughs from the crowd down below. Then, out of nowhere, he suddenly became somewhat serious, had completely changed his demeanor, and said something to me that I have not forgotten to this day, as we leaned on the rail next to each other, looking down at the stage and the crowd below.

"You see that guy down there mate?" he asked, in his Cockney brogue, referring to his former salon mate cutting the model on the long T shaped stage below. *"You know why he works* so *hard at what he does?"* Timidly, I shook my head *no*. *"It's because he's still trying to do the perfect Bob...we fucking all are."* They were profound words indeed.

With that and a goodbye slap on the back, he was gone. A ghost in the night; an apparition. He had left me with something that would give me cause to both remember, and, analyze in my head for many years to come; but quite frankly, I could give a shit less. I was hobnobbing one on one with hair royalty and loved it. I think of it to this day.

In my mind, at the time, I had become a reasonably accomplished hairstylist in my own right, and in a fairly short period of time, given the fact that I was only in the business a few years.

I was traveling and teaching, owned company stock, had position and title in a company that I loved working for, was making a name for myself, and had a hell of a thing going on. For me it was the stuff that dreams were made of.... but I was about to fuck it all up.

Sometime in the middle of the year, we got a transferee in from one of our salons in Ohio. Her name was Aninna.

She was half Polish and half American, having immigrated to the United States with her parents when she was three years old. She was a tiny little thing, with huge eyes, pursy Bardot lips, and a super fashionable fringy blonde boy-cut, that only very few girls could pull off. She had an ass on her that you could bounce a quarter off of, if your aim was true.

From the time that she had first walked in the door of the salon, I was mesmerized. Almost as if by premonition, I knew that I was going to get myself in trouble. Maybe God was testing me for weakness, as if he didn't already know exactly how weak I was when it came to the opposite sex. All I could think to myself was, *Dear Jesus, did I fucking need this further temptation heaped on my narrow little shoulders? I have enough shit going on.*

I didn't know *when* it was going to happen, nor did I know *how* it was going to happen. I just knew that at some point, somehow, this gorgeous little thing and I were most certainly going to be locked at the hip tighter than two beagles humping each other. It was just a matter of time and circumstance.

Fraternization among employees was always frowned upon in the company. Certainly, there was inter-staff dating that occurred, and provided that it was kept civil, low key, and didn't end up causing any kind of a stir within a given salon, it was, for the most part, accepted and overlooked, but, with the management and education staff, it was a different story.

If word had gotten out that anything of the sort was going on between a member of the management staff or education team and a salon staff member, you might as well kiss your sorry ass goodbye, or at the very least you would receive one hell of a reprimand, both written and verbal.

Shortly after Aninna's arrival, she had settled in, and had found an apartment that was not too far from the mall. She was soon traveling in the usual social circles with a few of the single girls from the salon, and making the nightly rounds at the local watering holes and night clubs that we all frequented.

I, of course, was also out and about on the same nightly circuit, and noticed that she apparently didn't date much, if at all. On nights out at one of the clubs or bars, she would hang out with the girls, loved to dance, and from what little that I saw, she would usually just have casual, fleeting conversations with guys.

She was quiet, and generally appeared to be somewhat shy, but unquestionably, she had a kind of stand-off sexuality about her that threw off vibes that said *if you want to fuck me you're going to have to work at it, and come after me...I'm not coming after you.*

I was not at the time looking for another wife, or for a full-time girlfriend...not by any stretch of the imagination. If it happened, then so be it. I just wanted to be free of the dysfunctional relationship I was in with Maria, yet I was wracked with guilt.

I knew damn good and well that I was the primary cause of all my marriage problems, and the bottom line was simply that I never should have been married in the first place. A friend of mine that I was at a bar with one time had even said to me, *"You're the original 'man who loves women', what the fuck are you doing married?"*

Guilt is a complex emotion. Before I even began what turned out to be an almost career-ending affair with Aninna, I had few scruples about cheating on my wife. I had done it before, had been with many women, and as I was traveling extensively now had a collection of *regulars* in each city.

For me, in my mind, the need for sex was nothing more than a basic human drive like hunger, but this time around, it was different. This time around, it was a possible involvement with someone from the salon staff, thus, the repercussions on all fronts would be staggering.

I had been sexually attracted to tons of women over the years and the thought of falling in love, either accidentally, or by virtue of an all out affair, never entered my mind. There are, however, times when two lives become entangled, and things simply get too deep. It is then that the unexpected happens, or maybe the involvement gets so deep that there's no escape.

There was something different about Aninna. She had a way about her, and an almost invisible sexual magnetism....it wrapped itself around you, capturing you as it drew you in, causing you to be both physically and emotionally aroused at the same time. Her overall aloofness to men offered a challenge, something I wasn't quite used to, since women gravitated to me so easily, but it was a challenge that I accepted. It tasked me, and it was something I simply had to do.

At times I would just stare at her and couldn't get enough…truly a danger sign that it was more than the potential of just sex. It was a danger sign that perhaps this time around, pure emotion and infatuation, maybe even obsession, might take precedent and certainly disguise itself as love.

I finally made my move on a snowy night after a gang of us had spent a few hours at the pub in the mall. Maria was off that day, and as it was past 9 P.M. and I was not yet home, she probably just presumed that I was out; nothing out of the ordinary.

It was a quiet mid-week night and the club wasn't too crowded, so the few of us from the salon that had gone over just hung out at the bar drinking, talking, and listening to the music.

Aninna left the club a bit early, around 10:30, only to return a few minutes later because her car was as dead as a doornail out in the parking lot. A few of us were still sitting at the bar when she came back in with the news, tears welling in her eyes, as it was an older car with repetitive problems, and had barely made it from Ohio when she first drove to King of Prussia to start her new job a few months previous.

I immediately volunteered to give her a ride home. One of the other girls from the salon who lived very close to her at one of the other apartment complexes said that she would pick her up for work the next morning, thus her car could be contended with then. During the ride home to her apartment, we talked. Prior to that, our conversations at the salon were minimal, and I really didn't know too much about her. Without question, I think she secretly knew that I lusted after her. I'm sure there were times when she probably caught me just staring at her.

As we drove to her apartment, she asked about Maria, and what was going on with us. She had obviously been told by the girls in the salon that it was a tenuous relationship that was on the rocks. I'm sure that she had also been further informed that I was one of the biggest skin hounds in the mall, and that she should steer clear of me.

As we pulled up to her apartment, she thanked me for the ride and asked if I wanted to come in for a coffee before I made my way home…but there was something different about the way she asked me. This wasn't your standard *thank you* with a degree of politeness thrown in for good measure…*it was the look*, and that look said everything.

I was pretty much an expert at reading looks on women, and it was as though her look that night in the car was saying *Hey, you wanna fuck me, I'm willing, but make your move now, or don't make it at all, and go the fuck home to your wife.*

With almost 40 years having passed, the rest of the night is a bit of a blur to me. Maybe my mind is just blocking certain portions of that night out because of the eventual trauma that eventually occurred with the ensuing affair that we ended up having.

I can remember accepting her invitation to go in, and I also remember a feeble attempt on her part to make coffee, boiling water in a kettle on the stove to make *'instant'*, as she didn't have an automatic coffee maker. Within probably 15 minutes of venturing into the apartment, we were kissing passionately, really going at it, and ended up in bed. Indeed, it was as mutual and consensual as things could possibly be. If by chance she was told to avoid me, it was obvious that she could give a shit less, and that she did not intend to heed any advice given to her by the girls at the salon.

It's odd, which memories the mind conveniently puts aside after so long, and yet will keep on the surface only those that are viable, or in some way, exceptional. In this case, the sex was indeed exceptional. I remember every little nuance of her body. She loved to be on top and simply pound the shit out of you, riding you with deep rhythmic thrusts up and down. She loved to give blowjobs, and I could tell that to her, it was an art form; light flicks of the tongue, followed by gentle rhythmic sucking, very slowly moving up and down with her tongue on the underside of your cock. *She wanted you to look at her* as she was doing it; to take it all in visually, and to get even harder and more turned on…she wanted you to never forget it. She simply wouldn't rest until you came in her mouth.

By 1 A.M., I knew that I had to get my ass home, as it was getting quite late. Maria would surely have been both pissed off and frantic, and of course, Aninna had to get up in the morning for work, as did I.

When I got home, Maria was in bed asleep. I had dodged a bullet, and the next morning, all she asked about was what had gone on at the pub the night before, and who was there. I informed her very simply and innocently that Aninna's car had broken down, and that I gave her a ride home. Maria was none the wiser, or so I would believe, and I could only think to myself that maybe she was just in no mood to play her usual game of *60 questions*. After all, she was used to all this by now.

As the weeks went by, Aninna and I saw each other secretly on as many occasions as circumstances would allow. Both my schedule, and Maria's, had changed a bit. Instead us now having 2 days off together, we now had only one. Aninna happened to be off on the same day that I was, and as such, we milked that situation for all it was worth.

Remember, there were no cell phones and no tracking software in those days. If it was the same situation today, I would get my ass nailed to a cross in a fucking heartbeat, but back then, I could feign any number of excuses as to where I was and what I was doing, whether it be during the day or at night.

On the days that we were able to meet, Aninna and I had non-stop sex. It was, a veritable fuck-fest every Wednesday, almost all day long. We just couldn't keep our hands off of each other, but moreover, we were falling in love...*or so we both thought.*

We were scheming as to what our next move might be, how we could break the news to all, and when and how I would leave Maria and move out. That in itself would have brought on complications, given that Maria and I worked with each other, not to mention that I had violated a cardinal company mandate.

Something else that was in the whole complicated equation was the whole *parent thing*. My mother and father, being the strict Catholics that they were, looked on divorce as an abomination, not to mention the fact that my mother was thrilled with Maria as my choice for a wife. She was cute, innocent, and accepting of my mother's sometimes overbearing and dominant *Italian mother-in-law ways*.

Without question, my mother would have been wild with me over our getting divorced. She would undoubtedly be upset with my overall behavior as well, as it was a side of me that she did not know about.

They say that men who have affairs, and thus think that they are falling in love because of their affair, are just part of a parade of fools. If that were the case, I was certainly at the forefront of the parade, twirling the baton.

Things slowly started to unravel a bit at the salon. Perhaps we were becoming careless and just didn't realize it. In hindsight, I guess I presumed that everyone I worked with was either stupid or naïve, and that we could keep the affair as secretive as possible until such time as we both decided to spill the beans, but of course not until after I had contended with telling Maria and made our separation official. That time frame never happened.

The few guys that I worked with in the salon and had stupidly confided to, tried to intervene and tell me what a *complete fucking jerkoff* that I was, that my whole career was at stake, and that I was flirting with disaster. You try to explain to them that you are falling in love, and they just laugh and tell you that you're *fucked in the head*, that you have a *dick for a brain*, and that it's all in your imagination.

Aninna had also been approached by a few of the girls, and given the third degree as to what was possibly going on. She was becoming a nervous wreck, in addition to becoming a bit of an outcast, based on nothing more than the suspicions and growing gossip. *We were getting ourselves into deep shit.*

Somehow, some way, despite both our best efforts, our stealthy affair was being exposed little by little on an almost daily basis, but we were unaware. Without question, there probably *were* times when we were careless. Love, or the mere supposition of it, will at times make you blind.

I saw it in the eyes of my coworkers, and I heard the whispers behind my back. I decided that the only course of action to be taken was to finally tell Maria, expedite our separation, move out of the house, and take it from there.

In my mind, the company valued me too much, and I had too many allies among upper management to be let go. *That*, without question, was the stupidest assumption I could have ever possibly made.

On a Friday night, I headed home after finishing my last client at the salon. It was a five mile, 15-minute ride straight down Route 276, and as I had not yet settled on exactly how I was going to tell Maria, I had precisely that element of time to decide exactly what I would say to her, and what approach I would take. I was rehearsing it in my mind. Scenarios of hypothetical conversation ran through my head…if I say *this,* and she says *that,* then I respond with *this.* There would be no need to be cruel, just be calm, factual, and tell her that which she should already know….that this marriage was a waste of time, and we both would be better off without each other.

In the latter regard, I hoped for the best; calmness and rationale' on her part, but I also knew she could be volatile. I knew that she could also be hyper-emotional, but what I didn't know, was that she could be suicidal.

As I walked through the door, there was an eerie silence to the house. Our two cats, who never greeted me when I came home at night, were in the foyer and seemed upset. I could see from the bottom of the five steps that led from the foyer and up into the living room, that there were no lights on, nor the usual welcoming sound of TV being on, which was highly unusual. The hallway light at the top of the stairs on the second floor was reflecting down the steps and into the living room. Something just didn't seem right.

I called for Maria and didn't hear anything. As I went up the steps that led to the living room, I could immediately smell a caustic stench that burned both my eyes and nose, and caused me to stop for a moment and gasp for breath. It became obvious to me that *whatever it was*, it was coming from upstairs. Making my way up the steps from the living room to the second floor, as I was about halfway up, I had a full view of the hallway at the top. I saw a smoking, smoldering pile of what appeared to be just about every piece of clothing that I owned on the floor.

I knew that the smoke was not the result of her having set the pile on fire, but rather some other instantaneous and not well thought out event of some other kind…an event of anger and desperation.

She had, without any working knowledge of what the end result might be, first poured ammonia on the clothing, followed by laundry bleach...a lethal chemical cocktail, which when combined together combusts into a thick, white, choking smoke that fills the air, and is quite capable of causing extreme physical damage if breathed in.

Perhaps in her mind as she was doing it, she was actually pouring the deadly mixture on *me*…purging her soul…a cleansing of sorts, ridding herself of almost 5 years of pent up frustration over not being able to control me. In any case, she had obviously had her fill with things.

As I rounded the corner approaching the bedroom, I didn't know what to expect or what I would find, but I knew that whatever it turned out to be, it certainly wouldn't be anything good. I expected the worst.

Entering the bedroom, I found her laying on the bed moaning and semi-conscious, but lucid enough to tell me that she had taken a mixture of pills earlier in the evening, and that I should be happy now; that I got what I wanted, and that I would be rid of her.

Needless to say, that was *not* what I wanted. I just wanted an amicable end to things, and certainly didn't think things would go to this extreme. I called the ambulance, which came in a matter of minutes, and the night took its course from there, as did the next day, which was one of the worst of my life.

At the hospital they pumped Maria's stomach, sedated her so that she could sleep, and informed me that given her suicide attempt, she would not be released until she had received initial counseling there, and would agree to see a psychologist. She would then only be released if someone from the immediate family would sign documents to take responsibility and oversee her at home…in this case, obviously me.

Returning from the hospital about five the next morning, I did two things…first I poured myself a shot of brandy to calm down from what had obviously been one hell of a night, and then jumped in the shower. Somewhere along the line, I think I smoked at least half a pack of cigarettes in quick succession.

The shower is, and always has been, my sanctuary, my respite. It's where I think, plan, make decisions, contemplate, and in this particular situation, I needed to clear my head, totally think things out and ponder the phone calls that I knew I had to make…first and foremost to Dave, the salon manager, to let him know what had happened and have him clear my schedule, then to my parents. I would then call Maria's mother. If *dread* has a middle name, in this case, it's called *fucked*.

Why is it that a man who is so very conscious of his mistakes is often destined to repeat them?

Sometimes you are searching for something that you can neither name nor define. You find it when fate plays its hand, and it often happens no matter how much you have weighed and plotted the future, as if some element of self-destruction was at play. As in the age old words of poet Robert Burns, "*The best-laid plans of mice and men often go awry.*"

Actions have consequences. Depending on those consequences, maybe you'll have an epiphany for the better, or maybe you'll have a metamorphosis into *being* someone better. There is also the possibility that maybe you'll learn to face your fears, and circumvent not only those fears, but the inevitable disruption that they can so often cause.

As the saying goes, *be careful what you wish for*...sometimes it just might come back and bite you in the ass. If you're lucky, it may ultimately bring you back to reality.

Chapter Seven
Saint and Sinner

The day after Maria's attempted suicide was nothing short of chaos. It was a day I would just as soon forget about. Even now, almost forty years later, I cringe when I think of it. I cringe at that which I caused and I cringe at what was *almost* the end result. Over what? *Sex.* What a stupid horse's ass I was.

The morning started out with my calling Aninna to inform her of what happened. I caught her right before she was headed to the salon. She was already quite upset, reacting from all the gossip that had been going on at the salon for days, as well as the pressure and questioning from the other girls. She was hysterical, crying, and frantic. She said she couldn't take it anymore and that we should both just leave immediately without telling anyone, and head to Ohio where her parents lived.

Her father owned an apartment that we could have, and she suggested that we could start fresh with a whole new life together. I explained to her what had happened with Maria the night before, that there was simply no way that our leaving together was going to happen, and that things had been put into play now that changed the whole equation. We were both stupid for even presuming that we could pull it off so smoothly without so much as a hitch.

To begin with, the consequences of just leaving so abruptly would have been earth shattering. Although I was, without question, the cause of all that had happened the night before, I was still responsible for Maria. Believe it or not, I *did* have a conscience. I still had my parents to contend with, as well. There was no way I was going to compromise my relationship with them by simply doing something as stupid and childish as literally running away. My father, in particular, would have probably hunted me down, come after me, and kicked my ass, even though I was almost 30 years old. It's an Italian father thing...*go grab'em by the ear, bring'em back alive, and kick their ass*, but of course, they'll then tell you that it's all done out of pure love, compassion, and getting you back on the right track.

The whole premise of starting over and starting a new life...with what? Who the fuck in the industry was going to hire *us*, after abandoning our positions with a major company and just walking away without giving notice, especially in light of the disruption that we caused at the salon. Under those circumstances, and with no references, I wouldn't get hired as a dogcatcher, let alone get a job in another salon, and in all probability neither would Aninna.

After I told her rather firmly, that was *not* going to happen, and explained to her why, she became about as pissed off as any scorned female could be, telling me that I ruined her life, and that I was nothing but a bastard. As she continued her tirade, not letting me get a word in edgewise, I simply hung up. I *had it* by that point. As far as I was concerned, she was as complicit as I was, so don't give me any of this *I ruined your life* bullshit.

I was knee-deep in things, and had way too much to contend with, starting with the phone call to David, the salon manager. With a lump in my throat, I called his house to inform him of the previous night's events.

David was a no-nonsense manager who was constantly diligent and protective of the salon, and the fact that it had become the number one salon in the entire chain. He was certainly not going to jeopardize it.

As I explained to him all that had happened, and that I wouldn't be in to work, he, of course, asked about Maria, and expressed sympathy and concern. At the same time, he told me flat out that at some point throughout the day, I was going to have to come in. He explained that he had actually been aware of all that had been transpiring between Aninna and I, and had been ready to confront me with it anyway. He was also obligated to inform Anthony, our Regional Manager, and as a result, Anthony was already on his way up to see me. Decisions would have to be made. As he was explaining all this to me, I felt as if my life was flashing in front of my eyes. *I fucked up*, in a big way, and I knew it.

There was a very good chance I would be jobless by the end of the day, my legacy being a career that had gone from 0 to 60 and then back to 0 again. I told him I would come in some time in the afternoon after checking on Maria's status at the hospital again.

I don't know what I dreaded more…calling my parents, or calling my wife's mother. Without question, neither was going to be pleasant.

The phone call to my parents was actually rather quick. My mother answered the phone, and I simply told her what had happened. Her response was typical of what I would have expected, given her infinite wisdom and adeptness at multiplying your guilt by a factor of 100, as all Italian mother's do. She knew when to be calm, or when to explode, and exactly what verbiage and tone of voice to use with me. In this case, she did indeed choose to be calm, and said to me *"Good Lord, what the hell did you get yourself into down there? Have you lost your goddamned mind?"*

What else could you do except bathe yourself in that shower of guilt that is heaped on you at the time, take it at face value with your tail between your legs, and swallow it like a man. My mother was the last person that I was going to disrespect, *ever*.

Cutting off the conversation quickly, I simply told her to stay put, that there was no need for her and Dad to come down, and that I would keep them informed. Perhaps later on in the week they could come down when things had calmed down, the dust had settled from this whole thing, and Maria was out of the hospital. That was the end of the conversation.

The call to Maria's mother was next. Although Elaine, Maria's mother, could at times be a bit of a ditz…an innocent ditz…she was a good-hearted soul who treated me very well, and she, like every other mother who had a daughter, was constantly concerned about her, especially given Maria's naiveté'. She was always checking up on our weekly goings on since day one of our marriage, even when times had been better.

I knew that she was quite aware of just how volatile her daughter could be, as she and I had discussed that part of Maria's personality before. She had always expressed to me that patience and rationale' was what always worked best with Maria, thus I didn't know what kind of a response I was going to get from telling her.

I explained the events of the night before, and at that point, she became a bit frantic. It seemed as if I just couldn't get the point across to her, that her daughter was going to be ok. She wasn't exactly hysterical on the phone, but was obviously very upset, repeating *"Oh Dear God"* throughout the whole conversation. I calmly tried to tell her that Maria had literally dodged a bullet, but her primary concern was that they wouldn't *"lock her up in the nuthouse"* for any length of time, and that upon getting out of the hospital, that she would get some help and return to normal.

She was emphatic that we make every attempt to work things out. As far as I was aware, she had absolutely no idea that my fucking around as much as I had was the cause of things, and if she did, she certainly did not let on. I couldn't believe that it wasn't brought up. Apparently, if Maria had previous conversations with her about why we were having problems, she chose not to mention that particular aspect of things.

Without going into detail, I told her I had things to tend to at the salon, and if she wanted to come down later that I could meet her at the hospital some time that evening, but would have to call her back first with a time frame as to when I was free.

By this time, it was late morning and I decided that it was probably just better if I went to the hospital later on and went right to the salon and face the music. I was exhausted from being up all night, but yet, given the course of events from the past 24 hours, I was so ramped up mentally I probably couldn't have slept if I tried.

I arrived at the salon around 1 PM and was stunned to find out that our Regional Manager, Anthony had already arrived, sent Aninna home for the day after handling her situation separately from mine, and was prioritizing me.

That walk back to the office with him leading the way was the longest 8 or 10 seconds of my life. I could tell by his overall demeanor and the look on his face from the time that I walked into the salon that he was not happy with all that had transpired. I'm sure that in his mind the last thing that he ever expected was to have to deal with a disciplinary action with me, of all people. I was, after all, one of the so-called *golden boys* of the company.

Closing the office door behind us, he got right to the point. He had spoken to Frederick as well as to Ron, the General Manager.

Luckily for me, the company was big on second chances...*real big*, especially when a primary employee was involved. They were very aware that human nature causes things to happen, and that even people of value, who would otherwise think soundly most of the time, are sometimes compromised by those things in life that just come along and cause you to stray from the straight and narrow.

He had already handled things with Aninna prior to my arriving, which was the reason she was already gone when I finally got to the salon. They gave her the chance to either resign, or transfer to another salon out of state. She took a transfer to one of our Ohio salons close to where she lived, and left immediately. She was simply too distraught to continue through the rest of the workday. I never saw her again.

I, on the other hand, still had my job, but, at Frederick's astute suggestion, was given a cooling off period of 2 weeks with pay, and was temporarily suspended from the education team. I would be able to return to the team at some point in the future when it was ascertained that things were reasonably back to normal for me.

Frederick had undoubtedly gone to bat for me, thank God, as he had always been one of my primary mentors and supporters since day one of meeting him and being chosen for the educational team. He was always the one to come up with a rational solution that salvaged situations, in particular, those involving primary employees.

This was one of those situations where I'm *guessing* that what was *probably* said, as my fate was discussed with his input, was simply, *"Let me talk to him and straighten his skinny little ass out, but there's got to be a bit of a price for him to pay."* There would be no free rides.

I'm sure that in the mind of management, my staying home from the road for a while, being allowed to thoroughly think out all of my transgressions, as well as not having any new assigned travel, would allow me to supposedly spend quality healing time with Maria and to work things out. They were presuming that I would come to my senses and make a clean return to the team.

It was an amicable arrangement...one that I had not expected, and which had frankly stunned me. That decision also told me that I did indeed have value to the company.

Regardless of the disposition of things, and regardless of the degree to which the company placed value on me, the fact of the matter was that Anthony, as Regional Manager, was actually acting much like a *capo regime'* from the mafia, telling an underling in so many words, *you've been warned.* With that being said, there would be no second chances.

The next several weeks were surprisingly calm, but not without their share of occasional angst. I faced my parents, and I faced my mother-in-law, as well as my coworkers.

None of it was easy. Maria's brush with death had a sobering effect on her for the most part, but after her return home, she was subject to deep depression at times, and the healing process between us was a rollercoaster of emotional ups and downs. She now completely distrusted me, and who could blame her?

We had good weeks and bad weeks. We would seemingly take two steps forward and all would seem to be progressing, and then for no reason at all, something would set her off and we would take one *giant* step back.

It was maddening, but I somehow managed to make the best of it once again, find solace in the creative part of my work, and bide my time. Without question, I could see the handwriting on the wall.

Chapter Eight
A Kind Of Normal

Several weeks had passed since the events that transpired had come close to costing Maria her life…..and me, my career. We were both back to work at the salon, and on the home front we were trying to work things out.

The parents had made their visit within a few days of Maria coming home from the hospital, and chided us to do our best to get along, let things take their course, and hopefully heal…something that was easier said than done. My frustration level was growing on a daily basis.

I was pissed…pissed at fucking things up, pissed at letting myself get into the whole situation, and pissed that I was now, out of guilt, stuck in a marriage that I really didn't want to be in, and which I had to put on a good front for, with both my parents, and, my mother-in-law.

As I stewed over this, my philosophy became simple. I would be a good boy while I was at home and in the salon, but, knowing that at some point I would soon be back with the team and out on the road again, there was nothing that said I couldn't have a good time, should circumstances prevail, when I was a thousand miles away.

I took my work as a national team member very seriously, thus it was absolutely necessary that while I was away I got my designated assignment done to the best of my ability, made it a point to not even think about fucking around with any female salon staff member, as well as to keep any *extracurricular activities* that might come along as secretive and clandestine as possible.

I waited about a month before calling Frederick up at the office and telling him that things were going smoothly, and that I was ready to make my return to the team. Really, that couldn't have been further from the truth.

I was starting to go a bit stir crazy from doing 10 hour days in the salon, having an otherwise mundane routine that consisted of just work and home, and putting up with my wife's bizarre up and down behavior.

In the month that I had been suspended, I missed a team trip to Florida as well as a very important team training session out in

Columbus. I had become used to the excitement level created by all of the travel I had been doing, as well as the creative comradery of my peers on the team. Although I had great relationships with all of the team members, I had developed very close relationships with several in particular...almost brotherly, in fact. Without question, *I needed to be back with these guys.*

Working and collaborating with them, in addition to having the constant mentorship and advice from someone of Frederick's caliber to constantly urge me on, push me forward, and continually teach me the ways of the business, was nothing short of rocket fuel for my soul, and without it, I was running on empty.

Undoubtedly, without the amalgam of all of those elements, I would regress, and I had fought too long and too hard to get to the level that I was at, given the relatively short time that I was in the industry and had moved up so quickly within the company itself.

The team was predominantly male, but as time went on and occasional additions were made, several exceptionally talented females were added from the ranks of all of the salons from across the country.

Each team member had been chosen not just for their outstanding ability behind the chair in the salon as well as for having a specialty that they excelled in, but also because they happened to have a special charisma about them that made people gravitate to them, and *listen.* That in particular, is one of the most important qualities that any teacher, no matter what their field of endeavor might be, has to have.

We were handpicked, we were indeed special, and we were lucky. I didn't realize exactly how lucky I was until I had made my return and saw how remiss I was without it all. Perhaps I had just forgotten. Perhaps I had just taken it all for granted the entire time.

In retrospect, that which we did out on the road was very much like being a small special forces team in the Army, out to do a job, take no prisoners, and return home safely. *Veni, vidi, vicie...we came, we saw, we conquered.*

The salons were notified of scheduled training events about two weeks in advance, thus, it having been on the calendar for a designated day or days, we were expected, and training time was allotted.

When we descended on a salon, you could both feel and see the excitement among the staff as we entered, fresh from perhaps a thousand mile plane ride. After throwing down our road bags, we would walk the gauntlet of salon chairs, down the main aisle of the salon, and it felt like a slow-motion dream…getting accolades and hugs from those that we knew, and experiencing the intoxicating rush of knowing that we were admired. *They wanted to be one of us.*

It was as if we were descending from the clouds. It was like a drug, sending you on a euphoric high, and for me, returning to the team at that time, *a kind of normal*, that didn't just feed my ego, but also helped to erase all of my guilt and pain, reassure me as to who I was, where I belonged, and *who I belonged with.*

We were there to teach, to inspire, and to give them the hope and reinforcement that there was indeed a *next level* to that which they had chosen as their life's pursuit, that they need not be anonymous in their creative endeavors, and that within the 15 square feet of individual salon space that they called their own on a daily basis, they too could be a star, if only for 8 or 10 hours a day.

About 2 weeks after having spoken to Frederick on the phone and assuring him that I was emotionally and mentally ready to return to my position and get back to work, he agreed that I could resume my responsibilities. I finally received notice of a team gathering. We were to report to the corporate headquarters in Los Angeles for one of our usual training and strategy sessions, which was going to be held the last weekend of the month.

I was excited, but also apprehensive. I was excited of course, to be back with the gang, but apprehensive because I knew that in lieu of my absence, there would most certainly be questions from the other team members as to exactly what had happened. Those few that were closest to Frederick surely had already been made aware of the reasons for my absence, thus I spent quite a bit of time pondering my potential responses for the inevitable questioning that I would be hit with upon my return.

As we were brothers in arms when out on the road, we were also brothers in so many other ways, so it was not unusual to verbally get your ass kicked out of nothing more than what might best be described as a fraternal concern for each other....true brotherly love.

I was especially close to two team members in particular, Reg and Gianni. Upon my return, as expected, both of them individually pulled me aside, questioned me, and spoke with me about just how stupid I was in doing that which I had done, almost compromising my career, and potentially risking everything I had worked for with the company. They knew everything that had happened. In speaking with them, they were blunt, but they also knew how to come down on me with a velvet hammer.... *I was a brother.*

Reg, who was Black, was probably the most philosophical of our entire group. He was the type of guy who could talk to you calmly, rationally, and with great skill in providing you with the reason that things happen, the manner in which you should have the strength to deter the negative things in life, and above all, the remedy.

He was self-studied in many different disciplines and religions as well as the humanities, thus when you had a conversation with him it could easily turn quite deep and be a learning experience that made you look deep within yourself and into the depths of your own soul, but, he could also be a person to not mince words and tell you to *get your fucking act together, brother*...and if he had to, he would.

If I previously had any degree of racial prejudice in my brain based on my conservative, Northeastern Pa. small town Italian upbringing, it was surely purged entirely from me, from the very first day that I met him. Working with him, talking with him, and rooming with him out on the road, we became as thick as thieves when we were together, and I loved him dearly.

Gianni, who was a few years younger than I, was someone whom I admired immensely, and in many ways I modeled myself after, both behind the chair in the salon as well as when I was teaching out on the road.

Born and raised in New Jersey of Italian stock, he was, in one phrase, a lady-killer that looked like a pugilistic version of Tony Danza with the added swagger of Chuck Norris. He had a fighter's flat nose, large hands, a large ego, and probably more notches on his belt in regards to female conquest than I had since my entire coming of age. Women would simply go crazy over him, no matter where we were.

He was a well-accomplished amateur kickboxer, and during those times when we were assigned together and working in a strange city, I surely felt safe in his company. The skills he had learned and mastered in the defensive arts also translated to grace and skill with shears in hand, and made him one of the most respected hair cutters in the entire company.

Watching Gianni cut hair was like watching DaVinci paint…but with an attitude. It was his stance, his intensity, and beyond the love of art and craft, it was a guy who loved women as much as I did. As the highest priced stylist in the entire salon chain, he had a tiered pricing system with quite a bit of freedom to charge what he felt a particular haircut was worth. I can remember very specifically asking him how he determined the price that he would charge a female for a given haircut. His response was everything that I expected it to be, given his ego, and he simply replied, *"By the size of the wet spot they leave in the seat when I'm done."*

We were not angels when he and I were out on the road together, whether it involved women or weed.

He had a contact in most of the cities we visited on a regular basis to supply both ourselves, and, a few other select team members who also chose to indulge, with *choice weed*. We kept it quiet and low key.

The company training facility and education center was located in Columbus Ohio, thus we spent quite a bit of time in that city, and it was resplendent with drug connections, as well as cheap strip clubs on the main drag. We drank, cavorted, and at times found girls that were willing to be haircutting models for the next day's training session, *and more*. Many times, more often than not, there was indeed, *more*.

When I made my return to the team, he made no bones about pulling me aside and telling me with brut logic *what a dumb fuck I was*. It amounted to this… *You could certainly have your side thing*, just use common sense, don't hurt the team, and most of all, don't hurt your family. What he also meant was *don't make a fucking jackass out of yourself.*

On my next trip to Los Angeles, I, along with Frederick and a few other team members made our way to corporate headquarters located in a magnificent office complex located just off of Wilshire Blvd. in the downtown area.

I was to have a brief meeting with the company Vice President of Marketing regarding the in-house product line, which I did all of the field-testing for. The meeting was brief, and as it was approaching 1 P.M., the senior administrative assistant and manager of the office pool informed us that we were invited to accompany Mr. Schwartzman, the Chairman of the Board, and Ron, the General Manager, to lunch at one of the swankiest Italian restaurants in the downtown Los Angeles area... *Ristorante' La Scala*.

This was not only one of Schwartzman's favorite haunts, but he was also one of their best clients, deserving of his own private wine locker....a privilege reserved for only a few select clients.

The restaurant was not only known for its gourmet Italian cuisine, but also for its flambé tableside cooking and overall exquisite food presentation.

After being seated by the host and ordering drinks, we were surrounded by a small army of waiters as well as the matre d', who was all too familiar with Schwartzman as a guest. Schwartzman simply said *"Georgio, take care of us."* It was his way of telling him to bring us a bit of everything on the menu, ranging from appetizers and pasta, as well as other accompaniments.

As we were waiting for what would be a continual flow of gourmet food to arrive and the conversation then began to flow, I suddenly realized by virtue of where it was heading that this was more than just a complimentary lunch with the powers that be, but rather something more; an ambush...*a sit-down*, aimed at me, but not in the typical sense. It was what can only be called, *an intervention*.

It was their opportunity to tell me face to face and with words carefully chosen, but wrapped in a cocoon of humor and smiles, and all done very tongue in cheek, that there would be no second chances should I repeat the error of my ways; that they valued me, but that I shouldn't take it for granted. Everyone, no matter who they might be within the company, was expendable. Although it was not said with those exact words, I got the point. It was a conversation that was both humorous, and, *serious*.

In essence, I got my ass handed to me before both the bread and the pasta even arrived at the table, and they made me well aware of things in the most amicable way that they could. It was all done with smiles, a few laughs, a reassuring pat on the back, and an undertone that said *we understand that boys will be boys*; but it also meant *don't let it happen again...ever...because the next time it does, you're fucked*.

As that day and that meal are both etched in my memory, I tend to think back on it occasionally and realize exactly why I loved the company so much.

It's rare that a company recognizes the folly of human conceit, as well as the fact that *artists in an artistic trade* are so often the ones who are most subject to falling down occasionally. Perhaps it is the nature of the beast as it applies to creative people in such a creative industry such as ours is, and that certain behavior could be looked at as being either that which is expected from the eccentric and artistic mind, or simply a careless lapse of judgement.

They wisely knew that when circumstances warranted it, that it was their job to pick you back up, dust you off, and push you forward again.

I went back to King of Prussia with both a sense of relief and a better sense of *self*.

I would not make the same mistake *twice*...but...that did not mean I had to continue in an unhappy marriage, nor give up the freedom to be me.

Chapter Nine
In The Midst Of Chaos

Chaos is usually the predecessor to change. Usually, there is an end to it, and hopefully a new beginning. It's only when the chaos ends and there is a temporary calm, but, the underlying circumstances have not changed to any degree, that it ultimately brings about *more chaos*. You know its coming, you know it is going to happen again, but you just don't know when.

More than a year had gone by since past events almost pushed my marriage, my life, and my career over a cliff. Somehow, I hung on by my fingernails, pulled myself back up by the bootstraps, and had enough mental wherewithal and rational thought process to prioritize where I was in life, what I had to do, and think about a remedy that would supposedly lead me to a happy ending.

It was the summer of 1981. Maria and I were getting along, but just barely. You could say that we healed to a degree, but really we were doing nothing more than treading water. We were at the point where we could function domestically with a minimal amount of arguing, and were reasonably pleasant to each other. Let there be no doubt, if there was ever a mutual bond as you usually think of it relative to a marriage, it was long gone.

Our relationship was much like two roommates living under the same roof together, both doing only that which had to be done to take care of the household, its finances, and everything domestic. Beyond that, there wasn't anything emotional or physical that would define it as a marriage, other than it being legal, and committed to paper.

Our once bi-weekly routine of weekend visits back home to Pottsville for Sunday dinner became few and far between, so needless to say, the parents on both sides were concerned as to if we were getting along, and if things were finally returning to normal.

The questions at times were endless, mostly done clandestinely with either of us, in a private moment with parents, but...*especially by my mother*. Both Maria and I put on a good front to keep all those concerned calm and at bay. There was no doubt in my mind that deep down they were all posturing themselves for that ultimate phone call at some point, as to the inevitable…that we had separated, and that it was over.

My mother was both tenacious and tough, but whenever a topic of some life altering event would come up, such as divorce, an illness that was life threatening, or death, she could only *whisper about it* and duck her head in the sand. In Italian, they would often refer to something of that nature as an *infamnia*, and to my mother, divorce was indeed an infamnia.

It didn't matter whether she was conversing with you on the quiet solitude and privacy of the front porch, or in the middle of the Sahara Desert with no one around for miles. It was a combination of her simply not having the stomach for it, and at times looking at a given situation with either great disdain or disgust. I'm sure that contributing to that as well, was her strict upbringing by my ever vigilant grandfather and his old school ways. He was always cautious that there might be someone listening to your conversation, thereby ending up with your getting the blame for having a big mouth, or for starting an unfounded rumor. He trusted no one, and had a saying which I remember to this day: *"I wouldn't trust the Virgin Mary herself, if she sat on my lap."* You were to be cautious of people, and were to avoid being labeled a gossip or a big mouth at all costs.

When I would be visiting Mom at the house, I might ask, *"So Mom, how's Mrs. 'So and So' doing?"* Her response was always typical if there was bad news….a single index finger to the mouth, making that *hush-hush* sign that we all know, and then a *barely whispered* answer: *"Oh, God, she has cancer,"* or *"Dear Jesus, her son got divorced, she's a mess."* Her responses were always whispered and never spoken out loud. Whenever I would hear my mother's reply that started with either *"Oh God"* or *"Dear Jesus"* I immediately knew that which was to follow…some harbinger of doom, or the possibility of a ruined life that would never recover and live in anguish because of illness, death, or a disgrace of some kind. To my mother, divorce was almost as bad as a death in the family.

In Pottsville, you could always spot the ones who were in continual mourning. If by chance you might happen to cross paths with them, you would not want to find yourself in a position of having to listen to them *again* for the *umpteenth time,* about that which they were still collecting condolences on, even though their life-altering event had happened years earlier.

They always had several tissues tucked up their sleeve, and were ready for a good cry if someone would listen, or, if they happened to see an opportunity that allowed them to shed tears and articulate the details of whatever had beset them years earlier. The fact of the matter was that in some ways they *loved* it, as well as the sympathy that you would bestow on them. They loved the martyrdom of the whole thing. It was as if *suffering* was their preordained lot in life and was God's will.

My mother had one friend, Mary, who was actually a distant cousin, and who had lost her son to a heart attack when he was just 42. When I would come back to Pottsville and would be back at the old homestead for a visit, I would occasionally bump into Mary, who would come over for afternoon coffee several times a week, *and then it would start* ....as soon as she walked through the fucking door.

"Oh God, honey, I haven't seen you in so long. Millie, Millie, he's so gorgeous with all that hair, he looks just like my Johnny. Oh God, it's been 20 years since I lost my Johnny." The tissues would be pulled out from under her sleeve, tears would start rolling down her cheeks, and with frail voice cracking and shaky hands, she would then come toward me with outstretched arms for the hug that she thought she deserved.

Of course, the silent unspoken response in my head was, *Ok Mary, we get it...the guy's dead...he's dead 20 fucking years, and you're crying every day for 20 years as if it just happened yesterday. Can we move on with it now, for Christ's sake?*

Truly, it's an Italian thing. Surely, if they would have had the chance for added drama at the funeral, they would have crashed through the traditional graveside wreath of flowers showing the time of death and throw themselves in the grave screaming in Italian, *"Mio Figlio, Mio Figlio"* (*"My Son, My Son"*)

The salon was doing very well, as it had since day one, but there were constant staff changes afoot. The changes were the kind that always comes with growth, and to some degree, there was a revolving door of personnel. This made for a sordid, and at times almost comical cast of characters who, as supremely talented as they may have been in cutting and styling hair, lent to the overall persona of the place... gay, straight, lesbian, Black, couples, and singles. We even had an absolutely *gorgeous* Italian girl, who was born in Italy and lived in nearby Norristown with her grandmother, after having being sent to the United States by her parents. She was staunchly Catholic, and made no qualms about saying that she was a virgin and was waiting for marriage to have sex. The other girls in the salon, all of whom had certainly been enjoying sex since their teen years at the very least, had a fucking field day with that one behind her back, but nonetheless, she was a good kid, respectful, and well liked by all.

My twisted little mind did absolute somersaults with the thought of nailing her, but of course, after the events that had transpired not all that long ago, I kept my cool, as well as my distance, as tough as it may have been.

The nature of the salon business is and always has been that of diversity in regards to the staffing process, and it could be said that those who are creative and possibly even gifted to the greater degree are simply eccentric or eclectic in their ways and thought. The best analogy that I could make is that it was like working with twenty Jackson Pollocks, all at the same time. You get used to it. You expect it. To some degree, even the public expects it. Creativity many times breeds eccentricity.

David, the stalwart and steady salon manager since its opening, had moved on, and I was named as one of two co-managers for the salon, in addition to keeping my position on the national education team.

Maria, in her supposed healing process, had slowly taken on a bit of a personality change as well. She suddenly had more confidence and had developed a bit of cockiness in her overall attitude, in the year or so since her suicide attempt.

I can only presume that she was as sick and tired of the limbo status of our relationship, as was I, and that she also had her fill of putting up with all my shit over the six years or so that we were married. We didn't really argue much, and would just go our separate ways on a daily basis, driving to work every day in separate cars.

I went out at night, and she went out at night. We did our own thing.

When I was traveling with the team on assigned weekends, I would occasionally call home in the evening to check on the status of things, see if there was anything pressing that I had to be concerned with regarding the house, or if there was any important mail that came. More times than not, there was no answer on the phone when I would call at 10 or 11 PM. I knew damn well that either she was out at a bar with the girls from the salon, or, Lord knows where. *'Touche'*, as the French say.

I was sure that she had finally worked up enough nerve to either have an affair of her own, or perhaps a series of spiteful one-night stands. I was at the point where I could only think to myself, *good, go find another guy, go get fucked, and let's finally have good reason to put an end to all of this bullshit, and get it over with.*

Maria *never* called me at my hotel when I was away, except for one time when there was a bad sewer backup in the basement, which was obviously something that had to be dealt with immediately, even though I was out of town.

What then transpired because of that *one phone call*, was the situation that finally put the icing on the cake, so to speak, and finally ended things.

I was up in Oneonta, New York with Donny, our new Regional Manager who had replaced Anthony, as well as with Reg, my colleague from the team. We had been sent up rather clandestinely, feigning the need of our doing a regularly scheduled education class for the staff. The reality of it was that bad reports had been coming in to the corporate office concerning Randy, the salon manager. We were actually sent up to scope out the situation, see if all the reports of his erratic behavior and mishandling of the salon were true, and if so, then Donny would probably be given instructions by Ron, the corporate General Manager, to terminate him.

As for the education class, there were three potential haircutting models waiting to be assessed when we arrived, and one of them was literally all over me from the time I walked in the door.

Her name was Maryanne. She was a bit taller than I was, had beautiful dark hair, and was somewhat full-figured, with huge breasts. Although she had dark hair, facially she looked something like a younger version of one of my favorite blonde bombshells from the 60s, Connie Stevens, complete with pursy lips and coral lipstick *ala Connie;* she was as hot as a pistol, in plain words.

There was no doubt in my mind where this was probably going, but needless to say, given the events of the recent past, I had to operate with complete stealth so as to *not get my ass in a ringer a second time*. I was not going to make the same mistake twice. She was putting the moves on me before I even laid my road bags down in the salon.

Prior to the class coming to an end, and because of some very direct and aggressive flirting with me on her part throughout the day, we had a bit of a secret chat, and she agreed to meet me at the Holiday Inn where Reg, Donny, and myself were staying that night. I certainly wouldn't have privacy in the hotel room, and there was no way I was going to compromise myself with the guys being anywhere near me, and seeing that I was getting together with Maryanne. I quietly snuck away and called the hotel during a break in the class, and as I was anticipating the possible course of events for the evening, got my own room, putting it on one of my credit cards.

I simply told the guys that I felt a bit claustrophobic in there with the three of us in one room, that I wasn't feeling all that well, and just wanted to be by myself and get some rest, given the possible events of the next day, whatever they might turn out to be…probably firing Randy. The *last thing* I did that night was rest.

Shortly before eight that night, the class at the salon was over, and Don, Reg, and I returned to the hotel.

We went to the hotel bar for a quick drink, and as I had specifically told them that I was not feeling well, I just had a quick shot of brandy and said that I was exhausted and would be retiring early. Maryanne was to meet me at 9 P.M. On my way back to my new room, I told the front desk clerk that *a friend* was coming for a visit, and it was ok to give her my room number. Remember, this was before the era of cell phones, so any type of secretive one on one communication between she and I was therefore limited.

Shortly after nine, and just as I had gotten out of the shower, there were two light knocks at the door. Still a bit wet, and wrapped in my terrycloth hotel robe, but with hair freshly blown dry, I checked through the peephole in the door, and it was her, a bottle of wine in hand.

Upon opening the door, my intention was to immediately ask her if she had any problems down at the desk, and if either of the guys saw her come into the hotel lobby area which was right by the bar, but she didn't even let me get the words out of my mouth.

Tossing the bottle of wine on the nearby bed, she then immediately wrapped both arms around my neck, threw a lip lock on me, and said, *"Oh, you dirty boy, you have some nerve starting without me, don't I get to take a shower too?"* With that, she began to undress, and had her clothes off in probably less than 30 seconds.

Grabbing me by semi erect cock, and holding on to it almost as if I was a dog on a leash, she then led me into the still steamy bathroom. Turning her head towards me as she led me in, and with a soft voice and doe eyes, she said *"I don't think you're clean yet, I think we have to finish the job."*

We showered and we had sex...two straight hours of sex. She was insatiable, and all she wanted to do was go down on me. It was as if she was obsessed with it.

After being in bed together for a marathon session of over two hours, and somewhere between fucking, drinking wine, fucking again, and drinking even *more* wine, we pretty much passed out; and then, the unimaginable happened.

A little past 11 P.M. the phone rang. Let me clarify that I was in a state of being mostly drunk, and barely awake; something you might categorize as *twilight sleep*, compounded by a bit of an alcoholic fog, as well as being completely spent from fucking her nonstop. On top of it all, I was on the opposite side of the bed from the left side nightstand that had the phone sitting on it.

I did indeed hear the phone ring, but it was as though it was in a dream. I just simply couldn't move fast enough.

For some reason, the logic of which, to this day I still do not understand, *she answered it.*

I don't know who was more stupid...she, or I. She, for answering the goddamn phone, or me, for not anticipating the possibility of it happening. Beyond the fact that I was drunk, it was highly unlike me, as a *master of covering my tracks*, to have not thought that out ahead of time, and for allowing it to even happen in the first place.

Amazingly, in a situation like that, adrenaline kicks in, even in that physical and mental state. Faster than I could articulate the words *"Maryanne, what the fuck?"* she handed me the phone and said, "It's for you." It was Maria. *Of course, it was Maria. Who in fuck's name was going to be calling me 11 o'clock at night, in my hotel room, in fucking Oneonta, New York, The Pope?*

As I took the phone in hand and asked Maria what was up, there was a long silence...and then she let loose.

"The sewer is backed up and coming out of the fucking basement drain in the house, and guess what? As sure as shit, when you come home, I'm out of here. Maybe you could share it with that little whore that you have in bed with you up there, you prick." With that, she hung up, and it was obviously not only the end of the conversation, but also the end of the marriage. Chaos...predecessor to change. *It is true after all.*

Not surprisingly, all I could do was feel my heart pounding against my chest. Perhaps it might have been worse if I didn't have the somewhat numbing effect from consuming half a bottle of wine. Propping myself up in bed, I leaned the back of my head up against the headboard, put my hand up to my forehead in utter exasperation, and simply began to think.

That's it...think. Think it out, stay cool, stay calm, and soon this will all be over.

As in the past, here I was again, pulling myself up from the cliff as I had done so many times before, and as always, I would get myself up and over, on my feet, and deal with the situation. Now all I had to do was stay calm, think intelligently, get myself pumped up, and run the last few yards of the marathon.

Even though the end was obviously at hand given all that had just happened, I pictured it going some other way. I pictured it more with the *ball in my court, and not in hers*; more of a calm sit down, with the both of us discussing things, and I being the more rational one. In reality, I had hoped that a calm scenario such as that would take place, and would end up with her agreeing that it would indeed be best if we split up. At that point, it certainly appeared that it was *not* going to happen that way.

As I gathered my wits, despite the *oh, fuck me* state of mind that I was in, I got up out of bed, threw on some clothes, and told Maryanne that she had to leave.

I had way too much shit going on, was starting to get the beginnings of a splitting headache, and in all probability, given the possible circumstances prevailing at the Oneonta salon with Randy the manager, would have to meet with Don and Reg early in the morning to discuss the disposition of things, and what would be done.

We had a job to do, and although *this time* I was in no apparent danger of my job being compromised because of anything that had happened that night in regards to my tryst with Maryanne, my first thoughts were to finish that which I was sent to do, and do it to the best of my ability.

The next morning, right after I had showered, dressed for the day, and packed, the phone in the room rang. I presumed it was Maria again, or possibly Don or Reg, but I was wrong. It was Maryanne calling and wanting to know when I would be coming up to Oneonta again. I was in a hurry, in no mood to talk to her, and told her that I didn't know. I feigned writing down her phone number as she dictated it to me over the phone, and prior to our ending the conversation she simply said to me "*The next time you come up, promise me you'll call me. I'll get the room if you're with others, and we could fuck all night; all I want to do is fuck you...can we do that......please?*" I promised her I would let her know, but honestly, there was a snowball's chance in hell that I would ever be sent back up to Oneonta again. That was the end of that.

I made my way downstairs to the lobby and met up with the guys, had coffee, and we skipped breakfast, as our priority was to get to the salon and take care of the business at hand.

Apparently, the day before, while the class had been taking place, Don secretly went out in the mall making the rounds and introducing himself to some of the various store managers, asking for a word in private. In the process, he was gathering information concerning Randy's behavior as a manager, as well as within the social circles of the mall itself. He spoke with several of the salon employees too, as it was initially phone calls from the salon staff to upper management at the home office that prompted our being there in the first place.

The reports were not good, and his reputation within the mall was that of being a *complete fucking whackjob.*

The prior evening, while I had been feigning illness in my room and indulging myself with Maryanne, Don had then reported his findings back to Ron, who in turn got Frederick involved in the decision making process, and it was decided that Randy would be immediately relieved of his duties as manager. Diane, who was the salon assistant manager, would temporarily take over. Randy would be offered an opportunity to return to one of the company salons back in his home area out in the Midwest as a staff stylist.

Randy, like I in my situation just a year or so previous, had been shown angelic mercy by the gods that sat in their leather chairs at the corporate office. He was lucky to have not been fired altogether. On our way to the mall, Don informed me of what was to come down.

Reg had initially flown into Philadelphia from Ohio, and he and I had driven up to Oneonta in my car, so we were free to go. There was really nothing in particular left for us to do. Donny had also driven up on his own, and had met us there, thus he was going to stay to see the final process through, and then leave once a smooth transition was assured. In my mind, I was grateful that I didn't have to deal with anything else that day and was free to leave and attend to my own mounting problems at home.

The ride from Oneonta back to Philly was several hours long, during which time Reg and I had time to talk. There is no doubt in my mind that he sensed that something was awry with me personally, as I was a bit quiet and distant, but he didn't push the situation. Rather than confide in him, I just continually directed our conversation to both company and salon related matters.

I was in no mood to get into it, despite the fact that he was one of my most cherished friends within the company, and probably the only guy who could give me sobering advice, other than perhaps Frederick.

Upon arriving back in King of Prussia, we went directly to the Philadelphia airport. Reg had called ahead prior to our leaving Oneonta, and was lucky enough to be able to bump up his flight back to Columbus to a departure later that same day before we hit the road.

I had been praying that he would be able to leave, as under any other circumstances I would have had to put him up at my house for the night until he could get a booked flight. With my home situation being what it was, that was the last thing I wanted to do.

My only other choice would have been to spill the beans, tell him what was happening, and then take him to a hotel. Quite obviously, having any kind overnight company would not have been the best of ideas under the circumstances of Maria and I squaring off with one another when I finally got home.

When we arrived at the airport, we said our goodbyes, gave each other the brotherly hug that we always greeted and departed with, and I headed back up I-276 to the house, which was only a half hour from the airport if traffic was good. I had no idea if Maria would be gone, or for whatever reasons, would still be hanging around. I had not alerted her to my early return from New York.

As I pulled up to the house, her car was parked in the driveway, thus I knew she was still there. I was sure she was either packing or perhaps might be on the phone with her mother, who had recently made a permanent move down to South Carolina with Maria's stepfather. Walking into the front door and into the foyer I found her, surprisingly, wet mopping the floor...a noble act in light of the fact that the marriage was without question *over*, and that she was planning to leave, but then again, she was always a fastidious housekeeper.

The only thing that entered my mind was that in some way, her cleaning the house was one last way of her telling me to remember that no matter how bad things were throughout the marriage, we never lived in a *shit hole*, and that she always kept the place immaculate. Perhaps, in her mind, it was to let me know that in her absence, I might be living in a bachelor's squalor, and that I would never see that degree of cleanliness again.

She was surprisingly calm. Perhaps she was just exhausted. She had called her mother to give her the news, and for whatever reasons, call it an act of benevolence on her part, or perhaps just not being in a mood to explain or deal with specifics, she apparently did not tell her mother the reasons why; she simply told her that it was finally over, and we were separating.

She apparently had time to think things out in the hours that had passed since the phone call to the hotel that started the beginning of the end.

We chatted a bit, with her telling me the specifics of the sewer problem that had to be tended to in the basement, went up into the kitchen, made a fresh pot of coffee, and discussed things, quietly and calmly. During the conversation, we both placed blame, but it never got out of hand. We were both ready for an end to the whole thing. We were both tired of it all, and agreed that I would move out and that we would sell the house, as neither of us had the financial means to buy the the other out, regarding the equity...we would just take things slowly from there, one step at a time. She would reside there until a sale of the house was final, and I would start looking for an apartment of my own. With that, it was over.

They say that when it comes to love and loss, acceptance is never easy. We can't make someone see all that we have to give, make them love us, or make them change, nor, can we force ourselves to love someone when it is simply not there. All we can do is move on and stop wasting time, and that's precisely what we did. The one thing that we *didn't* know, was that the next chapter of both of our lives and careers was going to change radically, and it was going to happen faster than either of us could have possibly imagined.

Chapter Ten
Adrianna

The weeks immediately following our agreement to split up went very slowly and in many ways were filled with a roller coaster of emotions for both of us.

For me, it went beyond guilt, confusion, or a feeling of final freedom. There's something about divorce and leaving an established household and marriage that makes you wonder about how in the end run you are going to be labeled or judged, no matter what the situation was that brought on the dissolution of the marriage in the first place. In future conversations discussed among mutual friends and relatives, both spouses would in some way be labeled as either the hero or the pariah in that which ultimately led to the end of things, and in many cases, sides will be drawn between both families.

I had been taking my good-natured time finding an apartment to move into, as a whole new consideration of personal finances would be put into play for me.

I would have to pay apartment rent plus my own living expenses, as well as continue to support the house and a good portion of its expenses, until it was sold. Thankfully, Maria had amicably agreed to split house expenses right down the middle. We agreed to pursue a mutual *no-fault* status as per Pennsylvania divorce laws at that time. There was a national chain of mall-based legal offices that existed in the 80s...they were cheap, and expedient in what they did. The whole thing ended up costing us a mere $180 in filing fees. It was all that either of us could afford at the time.

Both of our parents had been told that it was irrevocably over, and needless to say, they were not happy. Maria's mother seemed to be a bit more at ease with things than were my parents. She checked in with us once or twice a week just to make sure that things were proceeding smoothly, and generally, she let us alone and let things take their course. She, having been previously divorced from Maria's abusive biological father, had been through this before. She looked at divorce as there being light at the end of the tunnel after it was all over with, and a new start for her daughter. She was also there to lend support, as would be expected.

Maria did not get along with her stepfather, Al. As things were transpiring, he was not in a supportive role of any kind, he could care less. Being as aloof and uncaring as he was, he really never acted as a father figure to Maria or her sister throughout his marriage to Maria's mother.

Not only did he and Maria not get along, but he had a buck in the bank, owned multiple rental properties, and looked at himself as *the great savior* who rescued Maria's mother, as well as Maria and her younger sister, from a possible life of living on the street with only a cardboard box for a shelter, burlap bags for dresses, and rope around their waists to hold up their clothes.

Of course, none of that would have been true, but the guy was, from the little contact that I had with him since the beginning of our marriage, an egotistical, arrogant ass.

He was a tall, gangly son of a bitch…a tough, cocky, second generation German, but frankly, I didn't give a shit, nor did he intimidate me. I couldn't stand him. He was the consummate definition of the word, *prick*.

My mother, constantly the optimist, was on the phone with me almost every day insisting that there had to be some way that we could magically pull a rabbit out of a hat, salvage things, and once again be on the road to marital bliss, There was also no doubt in my mind that to some degree, it was to save her from the embarrassment of having a divorced son, God forbid. Make note, there is embarrassment, and then there is *Italian embarrassment*; two different things entirely. If you were to look at it on a cosmic scale, then *Italian embarrassment* is the supernova of all embarrassments.

It took a little while, but as the weeks went by, and Mom saw that both my mind and Maria's had been made up to finally split, she finally resigned herself to the inevitable, and became quite supportive, urging me to get it done and move on. She wanted it over with, she wanted me to be settled again, and in the big picture of things, wanted one less thing to worry about when she went to bed at night.

It took almost 3 months for me to find a place to live. I was taking my time finding an apartment, perhaps because of having the security of knowing that I already had an existing roof over my head and wasn't necessarily pressed for time to move, but also because good apartments in a good area, and within my price range, were at a premium. King of Prussia was growing by leaps and bounds, and both industry and housing were booming on both sides of Route 276. Apartments were getting more expensive by the year, and housing prices were going through the roof. Finding an apartment within my price range was no easy task.

As the weeks and months went by, it didn't take long for word to spread like wildfire in the mall that I was in the process of getting divorced, and with that, the inevitable happened. I was besieged with an absolute shit-load of females throwing themselves at me, all of whom had gotten wind of the fact that I was finally available. Many of them had no qualms about making me aware of the fact that they knew it. It was precisely what I needed to get my ass in gear and find an apartment. My head was spinning, and to put it in simple terms, the women were *coming out of the fucking woodwork.*

I finally settled on a beautiful one-bedroom apartment about two blocks from the mall.

Are you kidding? *Me*, finally turned loose with no wife, a.k.a., *stone around my neck*, and my own place? It was like when they finally let Morgan Freeman out of prison after having been incarcerated for 30 years, in the movie *Shawshank Redemption*. The very first thing he did when he got out, was to look up at the sky to see The Sun, *and it was still there.*

If my status of being one of the so-called *Kings of the Mall* had to any degree lapsed during those months of both work and marital related trial and tribulation, I was without a doubt about to reclaim my crown, and in a big way.

Over the years that I had worked in the mall, I had bedded quite a few of the crème de la crème of females who worked there, but not all of them.

Obviously in a mall, which is primarily a retail environment with tons of fashion stores staffed primarily by females, there is a constant turnover of store staff, and new girls are coming in all the time. You just had to *make them aware* that you were there, who you were, and *what you did.*

Without question, as one of the top hairstylists in the area, and also working in one of the area's best salons, I *always* stood a hell of lot better chance of getting laid than did a young twenty-something male geek who might, for example, be the manager of a *video game* store. While he might be busy getting a new piercing in his nose every week and embellishing his wardrobe of gothic black, I on the other hand, had *the look, and the experience*, and I knew how to use it. It was never even a contest.

Now that I had my own apartment, I was running wild. The approaches to me were plentiful, and I was with someone different almost every night; I literally lost count. Christ, it was like *The Running Of The Bulls, in Pamplona.*

They were all one-night stands. Maybe in some cases, I saw them more than once, but the fact of the matter is that they were the last vestige of what could best be termed my *hit list*; the ones that I simply did not get to for one reason or another, while I had the hands of an unhappy marriage choking me around the neck.

For that matter, at least half of the girls on that list, after I had finally been with them, were rather direct in telling me that they too actually had *me* on their own list of sorts. It was quite a switch on things; me as *the prey*, instead of me as *the hunter*. Frankly, I didn't give a fuck. Mission accomplished, no matter how you cut the cake.

I had a client by the name of Adrianna who managed one of the boutique clothing stores in the mall.

I had been doing her hair for close to 5 years. She had an absolutely gorgeous face, and was right up my alley size wise...about 5'1, 110 pounds, with short, very dark brown hair, and a body like a Greek goddess. She was of a rather exotic ethnic mix...Italian, Black, and a bit of Portuguese. It was a combination that gave her both facial and physical attributes that were nothing short of striking.

When she came in for haircuts, we always flirted with each other and inevitably the conversation almost always turned to sex in a kind of humorous, tongue in cheek way. She was not only a great client, but also, over a period of time, had become a very close friend and confidante. She was fun, she loved to laugh, and somehow all of those attributes overshadowed any lust that I might have developed for her. We occasionally hung out with each other at the bars, went out to lunch together in the mall, and were able to talk freely to each other in a truly personal one on one manner, during those periods of time when I was going through so much marital and job-related angst.

She in turn, confided in me about occasional boyfriend problems and all of the usual relationship anguish that females experience and go through. She was quite remiss about not being able to find the right guy, let alone a guy who cared, and who would become a true soulmate, as opposed to just being a lover.

Let there be no doubt that we had developed a trusting relationship with each other, and had no problem sharing many intimate details concerning both of our lives.

She of course, knew my wife by sight, from having been in the salon as well as occasionally seeing us out together. Maria, in turn, had seen her in my chair innumerable times as a client, but they didn't really know each other personally.

On one occasion she said to me, *"You know, I've seen you guys together now for Lord knows how long...as long as I know you, and I just don't get it. It seems like you're both from two different planets."*

Call me naïve, (which is hard to believe) but for some reason, I simply didn't give any thought to what may have been an underlying motive in that statement, especially given *my* experience in reading women.

I should have picked up on it immediately, but the fact of the matter is that sometimes when you are *best buddies* with a female, your vision and your thought processes can become clouded.

What I *didn't know* then, is that we were also about to become lovers, and it happened in the simplest way possible that two people who were such close friends, and who knew each other so very well, would end up in bed together.

She was in for her usual 8-week trim, and asked me if I had found an apartment yet, in which case I told her that I had, and she then asked when she would get to see the place. I mentioned to her that it was only two blocks from the mall. I had nothing on tap that particular night, and, since we were friends who hung out together so frequently, I told her to come over that evening to see the apartment, and that we would have a few drinks, talk, share a few laughs, and maybe watch some TV; nothing out of the ordinary for two good friends to do.

Adrianna's beverage of choice was always sparkling Italian wine, something that I knew from buying her drinks during those long nights of one on one conversation at the mall pub, where we would just sit at the bar and talk of life, love, and happiness.

As soon as I finished up at the salon that night and exited the mall shortly before closing, I ran over to the liquor store in one of the smaller plazas that was right by my apartment, and picked up two large bottles before making my way home. I was expecting her about half an hour later, as she too had to finish up work at the mall.

Almost 9:30 sharp, there was a knock at the door and it was Adrianna, bearing a beautifully etched bottle of imported Italian Anisette which she knew was one of my favorites. I was never much of a drinker, and always preferred the mellow high of cordials like Anisette or Amaretto. I occasionally indulged in good wine or brandy as well.

As she entered, she immediately made herself right at home, kicking off her shoes and heading to the kitchen. Looked around, she commented on how large of a space it was for it just being a typical one-bedroom apartment, and how beautiful the newly installed plush rug was.

She said *"Let's tie one on, I'm fried,"* and began to tell me about what apparently was a rather rough work day, as her Regional Manager had apparently popped in unannounced. He then put Arianna through an absolute day of hell, nitpicking every little detail in the store.

We poured our drinks, and before I even got halfway done with mine, she was pouring herself a second glass of wine, having downed her first one in a few gulps. We made our way over to the couch and turned on the TV, making light conversation.

There was something different about her that night, and at first I couldn't quite put my finger on it. She appeared to be in an almost dreamy, somewhat mellow mood, despite having had a bad day at work. It was as if she was looking to quell her anxiety, and wanted nothing more than to relax, unwind, find solace from the stress of the day, and put herself in some other place mentally.

As I was half reclining, half sitting up on the corner of the couch with my feet up on the coffee table, she positioned herself a bit closer to me, commenting that I needed a haircut, and began to twirl a section of my shoulder length curly locks in between her two fingers, making little spirals out of what was already existing curls. I looked at her, somewhat stunned.

In a way, it was no big deal, given that we were such close friends, and it was the kind of physical contact that I didn't necessarily consider out of the ordinary. Nonetheless, it was unusual for her, and a bit surprising to me. I didn't really know her as being the touchy-feely type, even though she was such a close personal friend whom I had spent so much time with on so many occasions in the past.

As I turned my head towards her, she continued moving closer, and by that time, our eyes had locked. I could immediately see that she had *that look*. It was a look that I had seen before, on so very many occasions, and with so many other females in the past. They were times when my own intentions were quite different; times when *I was the provocateur*, and when the circumstances as I planned and dictated them always led to a physical joining when I was with a female.

If there was any irony to that night, it is simply that it was the furthest thing on my mind with her. It was nothing more than a casual *nothing to do* type of night to be spent with a good friend.

She was not only getting a bit tipsy and glassy-eyed from having downed two glasses of sparkling wine in about 20 minutes, but without question, was also getting horny as hell. I could not only sense it, but I could also see it. She just had *that look*. Leaning in ever so slowly towards me, she kissed me on the lips…slowly at first, and then, more aggressively.

I was actually taken back for a moment….shocked to say the least, but still, almost as if by instinct, I began to respond in kind.

Without a doubt, I think that at that moment our minds, as well as a mutual feeling in our loins, met in unison. It was like *physical telepathy*, if there is such a thing.

The kiss that happened between us that night might best be described as an *eternal kiss*. Beyond the beginning of mere foreplay, it was one of those kisses that you never forget, think about not just in the moments immediately after it happens, or perhaps for days after it happens, but rather *for years after* it happens. It was a kiss, the memories of which, you will take to the grave with you as your last thoughts flash in your mind, and you take your last breath of life.

She knew that I was stunned, and there came a point of brief hesitation. We pulled apart slightly, looked at each other for a moment, and for all practical purposes, came to a dead stop; yet with that there wasn't a word uttered. We were undoubtedly having the same thoughts: *Do we really want to do this, and completely fuck up a beautiful friendship?*

So much of that night is indelibly etched in my mind, not just in the physical time frame of *how it happened*, but also in a virtual mental replay of everything *as it happened*.

It led to what was absolutely the best night of sex I had with any one female up to that point in time, and I remember it all. Without a word spoken, a mutual and consensual joining of hands as we moved to the bedroom, the both of us slowly undressing each other, and our eyes locking and not losing their focus for so much as a second. I don't think that either of us could believe what was actually happening. If anything, I think we both wondered why indeed it took so long.

She had one of the most magnificent bodies I had ever seen on a female. Her breasts were perfect...not overly large, but whose size was accentuated and made to look somewhat larger by tiny pink nipples that jutted straight out a full inch. She had flawless light brown skin, and much to my surprise, she was completely shaven down below.

She was the very first girl that I had been with who was completely shaven. At that time, it was a new trend for females, having begun in the late 70s and was just starting to come *in vogue,* as evidenced in many of the more popular men's magazines such as Playboy and Penthouse. Prior to that, most girls might have trimmed, but did not shave completely. I simply couldn't wait to get at it, and as I gently touched and caressed her there, I commented, *"My God, you're so smooth, it's like feeling silk."* Whispering in my ear, she asked me rather directly if I liked it, and I responded by telling her that I intended on *showing her exactly how much I liked it.*

As we stood there for a moment, gentle hands explored each other and we kissed. I could feel her shudder as I placed my hands behind her, and using my fingers, made a slow moving track of circles from the small of her back and progressing down to the cleft of her ass between her cheeks; a kind of standing foreplay, where mere minutes seemed like hours, and which you simply didn't want to stop...all before putting thoughts and actions into motion.

By the time we moved to the bed, what had initially been an evening of my having been caught totally by surprise, and not having any expectation level whatsoever, became one of complete lust. I was literally drunk with sensation, with her body, with the fragrant scent of her skin, and the way that she felt.

I was overwhelmed with her presence, and the sight of her naked in front of me. It did not take long for all of our physical motion to became one of our both moving in unison, as I gently laid her on her back, kissing her softly. I began to move slowly from her mouth, to her breasts, and then down to her belly button, teasing it with my tongue in such a way so that she would know that which was coming next.

Her response to my going down on her was almost immediate as I placed my lips over her clit and began to lick and tease it with gentle flicks of my tongue, and although she winced at first and took in a deep breath, I could tell that she was beginning to feel somewhat euphoric from the sensation; the heat, the wetness, the physical rush that comes from the visual, as she lifted her head off the pillow to watch me as I did it, and perhaps purposefully make herself more aroused. She let out a simple *"Oh God"*, and began to moan. Without question, watching someone that you want so very badly perform that most personal and intimate act of love on you, could in itself be the catalyst to the ultimate orgasm.

But if I remember any one thing about that night, it was the manner in which we were both so physically perfect for each other and the way that our bodies melded together...*the way that we fit*...curve for curve, bare skin against bare skin, and the absolute perfection of how our lips came together, and without rushing, consummated that which was almost five years in the making.

We moved in a harmony that could best be described as a physical symphony of sex that was like a classically composed masterpiece.

If nothing else, sexually we were perfect together, and beyond that, we were truly *making love*. It was slow, it was purposeful, and neither of us wanted it to end. We had sex for several hours before falling asleep in each other's arms. By 3 A.M., we awoke, and she told me that she had to leave.

I begged her to stay, but it was only several hours until the start of a new workday at the mall for both of us. In my mind. I knew that even after she walked out the door, I would be consumed with thinking about her...that my every thought would be occupied with her, and that getting up the in the morning and beginning my day would surely be nothing short of multitasking, as I thought about her while trying to get ready for work and make my way to the salon.

We began to see each other every day, and every night. The sex lasted for hours, and was nothing short of exhausting...fuck for two hours, take a shower together, fuck another two hours, and then shower again. At times, if circumstances permitted, and with my apartment being so close, we would even take an hour or two in the middle of the workday to leave our respective jobs at the mall, meet at the apartment, and simply fuck our brains out.

The whole thing went on for weeks, but as sexually compatible as we were, unbelievably, there came a point where things just simply began to unravel. *We had begun to stop talking to one another*...that is, *talking as we used to talk* prior to that first night that we had been together, and had broken the cardinal rule of being just friends who knew each other inside out.

She was pressing me to make a major commitment on a daily basis. It was apparent that it was what she had been looking for all along, and on my part, it was simply unknown to me, going back to the beginning of our friendship. *I was the chosen one*. I just really didn't figure that out over the 5 years that I knew her, and she never pursued it because I was married....she simply waited patiently for the right time an the right circumstances, almost as if she knew I would at some point get divorced.

I was simply not ready for it, especially in light of my having just gotten out of an eight-year marriage that made me rethink permanent relationships and the lack of freedom that always accompanies them.

When it ended, it ended with nary a word spoken, much as it had begun. We remained friends, and I would see her occasionally in the mall, as well as out in the clubs and bars at night, but our relationship had now changed in a big way.

In the weeks after, the few times that we saw each other and conversed, whether it be in the mall during the day or when out at night, our conversations were just not the same, and the manner in which we even looked into each other's eyes was different.

At times, I swear I saw the beginning of tears in her eyes. I don't know if it was guilt or sorrow, but the reality of things was that in the end, it turned out to be all about the sex, and nothing more was to come of it.

I often think it could have been more. Perhaps if I would have allowed things to take their course and had shed my both my paranoia and fear, today we would be married. There is indeed every possibility that truly, she was my soulmate, and I just stupidly let it go and did not recognize it for what it was. However, fate had dealt its hand. Conceivably one could say that it was the *right girl* but at the wrong time, and for me, it was indeed the *wrong time*.

Ruining that deep friendship had a profound effect on me. I was starting to get tired of it all. I was tired of the whole lifestyle, even in light of the fact that my initial reasoning for not following through with a full-blown relationship with Adrianna was the potential lack of freedom, and of being trapped again. I was now having second thoughts about my entire way of being, and of my relationships, or lack of, with women in the past. Logic is sometimes not only buried deep in your mind, taking a while to come to the surface, but in your soul as well.

Although I was not ready to settle down again, my mindset was changing dramatically, and for the first time in years, I took a break from the whole scene, as well as a good long hard look at myself.

I actually went a number of months without any intimate female physical contact after my breakup with Adrianna, and if I went out to a bar a few times a week, it was to just sit quietly, enjoy a drink, think, and reflect on things, as I watched other *would-be kings*, confident that they were master of all they surveyed, go about their games of conquest, much as I had done....the pitch, the pose, the talk. In watching them, I was looking at my former self. Most of them were mere amateurs by my standards and experience, and from what I saw and observed, they didn't stand a chance of getting laid.

As I would listen within earshot just a few bar stools away, I could only think quietly to myself, almost as if I was a would-be mentor. *Christ, you're doing it wrong. Is that the best you've got? You need to say this; you need to say that. You're blowing it, pal. She's going to tell you to fuck off, and you're going to end up going home by yourself tonight, you dumb shit.*

What these guys didn't know is that somewhere along the line, things are going to change for them, *but have your fun now, because although you don't realize it, youth is fleeting, the clock is ticking, and nothing...nothing stays the same.* It's all going to come to an end, perhaps in five years, or ten years, or maybe it might even happen out of the blue next week. *This thing* somehow just hits you and you decide right then and there that it's time to pack it all in, that it's all bullshit, and that secret somewhat domestic and monogamous side of yourself finally makes an unannounced appearance, and tells you that it's time to be with just one person, and one person only, and to do it the right way.

I was now in a self-imposed pattern of chaste behavior. I had literally put myself in prison, and without question, it served the purpose of clearing my head. The only question now was, how long would it last?

April, 1983. Spring was in full bloom. I had stepped out of salon management, was still traveling with the national education team, but of my own doing, was not traveling with the same frequency as before.

We now had salons in almost every state in the country and although my travel had slowed down substancially, what little of it I was doing, I still loved. The company's expansion continued to take it to many other major metropolitan markets on both coasts, and with it, the opportunity on my end, to travel to new cities.

I loved the West Coast, California especially. When I was assigned to do a seminar there, visit a salon, or have a meeting at the corporate offices in Los Angeles, I would marvel at the culture there and all that it had to offer. It was radically different from anything on the East Coast.

Given my great love for New York City, it too, was an equal choice for a possible permanent move.

With so much free time now, I had started to go into Manhattan several times a month. I had previously been going in for advanced schooling on my own at least two times per year, but now, with so much time available to me, I was going in almost every weekend just to be there. enjoy myself, experience the city, and in many ways, clear my head.

Through those repeated visits, I developed a great yearning for its lifestyle and all that it offered. It was a combination of stimulating, exciting, and to some degree, emotionally exhausting, and New York could do it all to you within the framework of 24 hours, but I loved every minute of it.

I found out about what it takes to live and work there. Then as now, for all the young Turks trying to carve out their niche there, survival is sometimes fleeting, and in some cases requires multiple jobs to stay afloat. It could easily be said that 9 to 5 in New York City is a completely different experience, compared to what 9 to 5 is in any other American city.

New York had become like a drug to me. The city that never sleeps has a way of seducing you with its pleasures; pleasures that range from the artistic, the visual, and the avant-garde, to that of guilty and sinful. I loved to sit in Bryant Park and people-watch, but moreover, I loved watching the diverse mix of women that I would see. It filled a void for me, even in lieu of my lifestyle having changed considerably in recent months. The pleasure that it gave me instantly eradicated the occasional depression that would beset me.

Perhaps it was that I had not really been with another female since my affair with Adrianna, or perhaps I was beginning to experience what one might call withdrawal from what had previously been my constant need for sex, as well as the imprisonment I had self-imposed on myself. With each visit, I began to feel a stirring inside me.

Although the city placated me emotionally to some degree, and in many ways expanded my thought processes about so many things, it was also starting to bring back a sexual reawakening in me, one which I knew I would have to keep under control and find a middle ground for, given all of the women that were apparently available at any given time. It was a city where just the smell in the streets was enough to arouse all of your senses.

I had found a little bohemian café down in Greenwich Village called Café' LaMond which I started to frequent quite a bit during my weekend stays, and soon began to make a circle of friends there from the eclectic tribe of regulars who made it their regular haunt…writers, artists, musicians, and people from within the fashion industry, including a bevy of aspiring young models.

Little by little, I began to feel like myself again. I had found a group of peers that shared stories of their lives with me, as did I with them. We talked of our struggles, our relationships, and of how as artists we sometimes had to suffer through the pain of anonymity and the price that we had to pay for the sake of our respective art.

It was there that I met Meeka, and I was about to be introduced to a world of pleasure that I never even knew existed.

Chapter Eleven
1983 - Meeka / New York

In early June of 1983, I was in New York for what was to be my first photo shoot since entering the business almost ten years earlier. Although I had accomplished quite a bit since entering the industry in 1974, the one thing that had eluded me was photo editorial work. Editorial work, both then and now, is something which could very easily catapult you to the forefront of the business if circumstances are right, and also create an added demand for you to do things such as high paying product endorsements for manufacturers.

Although I was still relatively young in the business, because of my long term career aspirations, the mere premise of it at the time was exciting. *Fuck this mall salon shit.* I wanted more. I might have been a local celebrity of sorts in the suburbs of Philadelphia, but in the salon industry, you needed to be *published.* I started to realize that I was nothing more than a big fish in a small pond in King of Prussia. If I could slowly work my way into the New York scene of agencies and photographers, it could change things dramatically for my entire career.

I was starting to get my stride back, in more ways than one. The sea of emotional instability that had been drowning me in the past weeks and months was slowly releasing me, and I was beginning to swim to the surface to breathe. Although I had been castrated by the depression that beset me because of all that happened with Adrianna a few months previous, New York and all of its possibilities was certainly starting to reverse all of that. Every time I ventured there, I felt as if I had been given what could only be described as an adrenaline cocktail that *gave me my balls back* in more ways than one.

I had become very friendly with an up and coming fashion and editorial photographer who was originally from Panama. His name was Louis. He was a recent graduate from the New York University School of The Arts, and was connected to a number of the better-known modeling agencies in the city, as well as to the editorial departments of several of the major fashion magazines.

On one particular Saturday in early summer, Louis and I were to meet at the café at 1 P.M. to discuss a photo shoot. I had taken an early bus into the city that morning and was able to get an early check-in at my regular hotel, The Wellington on 7th Avenue. I took a cab down to The Village and just wanted to hang out for a while, see if any of my new friends were around, and get into my New York frame of mind.

I arrived at the café almost an hour early with the intention of just sitting there, relaxing, and looking for good conversation. The place was quite busy with no table seats available.

After I got my double espresso, I was awkwardly looking around with coffee in hand, making a decision to either stand, or take myself outside to sit at one of the sidewalk tables and enjoy the sun. A female voice with an accent was beckoning me from behind. *"You...I know you. You look lost, yes? I see you here many times."*

Her accent perplexed me. It was an accent that had me guessing as to where it emanated from. As I turned to see who it was, I saw that it was coming from a diminutive little dark haired beauty with a gorgeous smile, whom I had seen at the cafe many times before, but had never met. She was, to some degree, a *Bettie Page lookalike*.

She acknowledged how unusually crowded it was for a late Saturday morning. *"Sit my friend, or you may stand forever."* Both her incredible soft voice, one that could best be described as liquid velvet in its tone, as well as her somewhat undefinable accent, drew me in as much as her entire look and persona. She was of slight build with long, black, straight hair to the shoulder, uber short bangs cut straight across that said she was not afraid to be rebellious, and welcoming blue eyes that were like limpid pools that you could see your reflection in if the light was just right.

Although I had seen her there before, for some particular reason, perhaps because I was now in such close proximity to her one on one, I was awestruck, and in looking at her face to face for the very first time, her saw just how visually striking she was.

In my mind, I questioned why I had not paid attention to her during those times when I had previously seen her there, but then again, New York has a way of doing that to you.

In a city that is so visually multitasking, and where as you walk the streets your mind tries to process and sort out the emotions and sensory perception of several different beautiful women walking towards you at the same time, surely some will be missed. At that same time, you may also be occupied with feeling either compassion or anger at the ground-dwelling homeless, or legions of those looking for a handout. It can easily be said that you simply can't take in and prioritize all that is coming at you at one time.

As I sat down, we formally introduced ourselves to each other and gently shook hands. Her name was Meeka.

As our hands came together, the first thing that I noticed was that her skin was so incredibly soft I almost didn't want to let go, and as we released, I actually found myself becoming aroused by her mere touch. There is something about *first touch,* no matter in what form it may take, that makes it sometimes generate lustful thought processes that may actually supersede the visual element of things, or at the very least, bring an amalgam to all the other senses combined.

My inner nature took over. In a matter of a few seconds, I began to visualize flashes in my head and to fantasize. Her, naked. She and I, physically entwined in bed, and making love. My old self was coming to the surface once again, and I let it have free reign for the first time in several months without fighting it.

We began to converse. She was 25 years old, a photographer, and after having graduated from one of the most prestigious art institutes in Brazil, The Art Institute of the University of Rio de Janeiro, she came to New York to find her fame and fortune.

She was currently working as an administrative assistant at an art gallery that was on Prince Street in SoHo, and was also a master yoga and Tai Chi instructor at a high-end health spa and fitness club located just south of Midtown in Chelsea. In the meantime, she was putting together her first series of photos in the hope of finding sponsorship for what would then be her very first gallery showing.

Her accent was Russian, but with a few other influences as well. Although she had actually immigrated to the United States from Brazil, her parents had fled the Soviet Union for Poland when she was 5 years old. Her father was an engineer, and two years after the family had settled in Poland, he was offered a job as a project leader for a large engineering firm in Sao Paulo, Brazil, which is where they ended up settling.

She immediately fascinated me from the time I turned and saw her sitting alone at a small two-seat table less than three feet behind me.

Women of any geographic persuasion other than American, in particular, women from either Europe, the Baltic, or South America had *always* fascinated me, as they seemed to have a way about them, an intelligence and worldliness that was somehow lacking in the American women I had been with in the past, and they were usually bi-lingual. In this particular case, Meeka not only spoke her native Russian, but was also fluent in Polish, Portuguese, and a little Spanish, as you would expect, given her moves since childhood.

As she lit a cigarette, blowing the smoke up and away so slowly and purposefully, she then asked about *me*. Her English was good, but accented...broken somewhat of course, and missing the subtle nuances that would otherwise cause you to say that she was 100% fluent.

"*So, you....what you do? I see you here many times, but we never talk before.*" I explained to her that I was a hair stylist, that I was from the Philadelphia area, and that I came into the city quite often for both pleasure and work, and in this particular case, was here to discuss a photo shoot with Louis.

She looked me straight in the eye and without even flinching, she then said "*Ahh, so...you are 'larilas' ?*" I looked at her quizzically as I attempted to both repeat the word, and with my tone and voice inflection, question what it meant. *Larilas* was apparently Portuguese slang for *gay*.

She smiled, taking another drag from her cigarette and repeated herself. "*Larilas...how you say? Gay?*" I explained to her that, no, I was not gay, and that if I was in my art and trade for any one reason, it was because I loved women so much.

She then asked me what kind of women I liked, and I instinctively gave her a tailored response using adjectives that would not only stroke her female ego, but could have also been me describing *her*.

In a way, I felt like I was being both seduced and coerced into giving her not just the right answer, but also, the answer that she wanted to hear.

We had a few moments of awkward silence. She smiled as she sipped her espresso, appearing to be studying me to some degree.

"I think you have a secret, yes?...all men have secrets, am I right?" I smiled, and was actually a bit shocked at both her bluntness and aggressiveness in our conversation, but at the same time, I was also stunned at what might best be called her clairvoyance.

I asked her what made her think that I had some sort of secret. I felt as if she somehow saw right through me, and knew my history. It was as if she had read me, and simply ascertained that my coming into New York was the act of a wayward soul with a past; one who sought sanctuary in the city of dreams.

I was somewhat curt and defensive, but yet shy in my response, and told her that I was separated, and in the process of a divorce; that I simply come into the city as a welcomed escape; to relax, clear my head, and to hopefully practice my craft in a more fulfilling way.

Noticing that her leather bound portfolio was resting against the chair just underneath the table, I asked if I could see it. *"I will show it to you, but I will also see your eyes."* At first, I did not understand what she meant. Finally, it dawned on me that what she was alluding to was that I dare not humor her, or tell her how good it was out of nothing but politeness. If I did have an eye and a passion for her art, in whatever form it was, within the pages of that red leather portfolio, she would know it immediately. With that, she handed it to me. She didn't say a word as I opened it and turned the pages. She was looking at *my eyes*, studying my visual responses, and perhaps in doing so, it was a first test of some kind for me.

Truly, she would not be placated. I chose my words carefully as I gazed at the photos, and in commenting on each one, was extremely cautious in using the right verbiage that only fellow artists would use to convey approval to each other.

I knew that if there was even the remotest possibility of my ending up in her bed, it would not happen, regardless of any attraction she might have for me, unless she felt that I was telling the truth. Without question, a relationship with a girl of this type would most certainly be as cerebral as it would be physical or lustful.

She did not give herself away in any way, shape, or form. If she was going to fuck you, it was going to be all-consuming, both physically and mentally. For her, sex and lovemaking would need to have a purpose, in addition to being totally self-ingratiating.

The portfolio was truly an eclectic mix of mostly black and white nudes that were both artful and erotic, with a heavy focus on the human form, and with superb use of lighting. Some of the photos were male nudes, others were female, and yet others were of couples joined in the unison act of making love, but shadowed and artful to the point that you certainly could not call them pornographic. They were beautiful.

Quite obviously, her appreciation of the human body was on multiple levels. It was almost logical that someone who was a master of yoga and Tai Chi was going to have an eye for the human body, and be able to transpose it to art. For that matter, a female such as she, who had such an eye for the erotic, would insist that if indeed she fucked you, that the visualness of whole act itself would need to have the same element of lust to it as what you saw in the rawness of her photography. It would have to be as if she would be posing artistically for one of her own photos while she herself was having sex. Undoubtedly, she would want being with her to be something that a lover would never forget.

As she had mischievously asked me about my supposed secrets when I first sat down, I now questioned in my mind what secrets *she* might harbor.

She had obviously shown me the portfolio for reasons beyond that of two creative artists sharing. There was no doubt that in some way she was communicating something else to me, perhaps an attraction for me, but for the time being, it was to remain unspoken, at least until she made a decision of whether I was worthy or not, and whether I was her kind of man.

With carefully picked words, combined with emotion, and the physical movement of how both my hands and voice would convey, I simply told her, *"You have a gift...you tell a story with your work."* Resting her chin on folded hands, smiling at me, and with her elbows casually propped on the table, she said, *"I like you. There is no, how you say in English? Bullshit? I think you speak from the heart. I can see it in your eyes ...we should have talked. long ago."*

Almost as soon as I had finished leafing through the last page of the photos, Louis came through the door with apologies for being late because of the Midtown traffic, and not being able to get a cab. Honestly, I hadn't noticed. I was simply too engrossed in Meeka.

I was once again smitten…this time, by a voice, a beautiful face, and a female aura that shone on me with a brightness that could have easily blinded me….*again.*

With that, Meeka abruptly stood up, gathered her things, and said, *"My hair, you will cut it? I can see that you have passion. You call me next week?"*

Pulling a pen out of her purse, she gave me a business card for the gallery and on the back of it wrote her apartment phone number and address as well. She lived in SoHo.

Looking at me and smiling, she then said, *"You have no meat on your bones, but that is good for yoga. You come, cut my hair, and I will show you yoga, and show you all the things you didn't know you could do with your body because of it."*

I agreed, told her I would absolutely love to cut her hair because she had such an exotic look, and told her I would call her by mid-week to confirm things before coming back in the following weekend. As I stood up to see her off, she kissed me lightly on each cheek in the European style of both hello and goodbye, and with that, using her thumb and forefinger, wiped away a lipstick smudge which she had left in saying her farewell.

As she left and exited through the glass door at the front of the café, I watched her until she crossed the street…half running, half walking, in the same hurried manner that every other New Yorker does because of a lifestyle that is usually dictated by commuter time restraints and places to be. I watched her until she was out of sight.

Louis sat down and we began to discuss the details of the photo shoot, which surprisingly, he had set up for Sunday, the next day, but my mind was really a million miles away. I knew that the coming week and the anticipation of having to wait a full 7 days to see Meeka again would certainly be more than I could bear. Once again, the demons were playing their hand…*or were they?* Maybe, this was something else…something different.

The following day I met Louis down in The Village around nine in the morning. We were doing our shoot at an old apartment which I found out later was where the iconic comedian from the sixties, Lenny Bruce, had once lived during his short, but none the less controversial, career. Our model for the day was a gorgeous Italian girl by the name of Isabella.

At age 19, she was new to the business and as such, Louis was able to get her for the shoot by virtue of her agency still wanting to build her portfolio before hiring her out for paid assignments.

It was going to be what in the business is referred to as a *trade for print shoot,* meaning simply that you were not paid. You do it for gratis copies of the prints in order to build your portfolio, and have something to show when you finally did go on an interview for a paying job. This applied not just to Isabella as the model, but also to the rest of us as independents that were partaking in the shoot that day, inclusive of myself as the hair stylist, the makeup artist that Louis had recruited, and the wardrobe stylist.

The shoot went well but was exhausting, and we were working under time constraints for lighting. Isabella was far from modest. Although the wardrobe stylist had everything set up for clothing changes in one of the side bedrooms of the apartment, Isabella had absolutely no qualms about making quick changes just a few feet away from the shot setups.

At times, for a brief few seconds, she was naked with her back turned to us as she quickly changed from one outfit to another with the assistance of the wardrobe stylist. She was obviously used to it, as part of that which she did as a model. In the world of modeling, there is no room for modesty, whether it was backstage at a runway show or for a simple shoot such as the one that we were doing that day.

Wrapping up the shoot by 6 P.M., I gathered my things, and luckily, was able to catch a cab up to the Port Authority and grab the 7 P.M. bus to get back home.

Although the salon and my clients would be waiting for me once I returned, there was no doubt in my mind that for the duration of the coming week, I would be preoccupied with Meeka in such a way as I had not been with any other female in quite some time.

Chapter Twelve
An End, And A New Beginning

I arrived back home to King of Prussia late Sunday night. Monday I was off, and I could relax a bit and get some errands done prior to returning to the salon early Tuesday morning. I had checked my salon booking schedule just prior to leaving for Manhattan, and knew that I had an extremely busy week behind the chair. Although I was very much preoccupied with the thought of the following weekend with Meeka, I was still very much devoted to, and prioritized, that which kept me financially afloat...doing hair. The industry was always my first and foremost mistress, and as such, I was always guarded and conscious of the lifestyle that it gave me.

The salon at the mall had itself changed dramatically over a period of almost 10 years, as had the company on a whole. Many had come and gone on all levels. I, as well as the core members of the education team such as Frederick, Gianni, and Reg, remained in place, guarding and vigilant to all that we had worked so hard to build and achieve over almost a decade.

I was still the primary education force behind the ever-growing product line, and as a result, both sales and public exposure to it had increased dramatically because of my efforts.

Things were good, and although I had stepped out of management and to some degree, company education, I was still quite busy, not just with my clientele at the salon, but also acting in an advisory capacity on certain matters to those that I answered to at the corporate office in Los Angeles as well. In addition, I would occasionally accept a seminar assignment if it didn't interfere with my going into New York, and if it only involved relatively simple local travel of perhaps 100 miles or less. I hated extreme distance driving, where you had to be out on the road driving for hours at a time.

I was finally getting settled into a whole new routine and the beginnings of a whole new life. With the divorce pending, and thus being *almost* single again, having my own place, and going into Manhattan on a regular basis, I was now content for the first time in years.

Without a doubt, both of my parents breathed a great sigh of relief as well. They were relieved that my divorce from Maria was proceeding smoothly without any major arguments. My mother would often say to me in Italian "*Tu contento, mi contento*" which simply meant, "If you're content, I'm content."

Maria and I were actually on quite amicable terms and would meet weekly to take care of the house finances and related matters.

A few weeks previous, we had finally found a realtor that we were both satisfied with, the house was listed for sale, and it was being shown to prospective buyers. Maria, in the meantime, had finally found a boyfriend.

He was from the Kazakhstan area of Russia, and in 1983 prior to the end of the Cold War, it was still technically part of what was then the Soviet Union.

He, his parents and his brother had made their way to the United States, first attempting to settle in New York City, and then ultimately ending up in Philadelphia, in an area called Fish Town…an emerging neighborhood which was a mix of Middle Eastern, Southern European, and Russian.

I had met him only once when Maria came to my new apartment to pick up some lamps that I neither wanted nor had room for. I could see immediately that he was a smug, arrogant, controlling son of a bitch. Without question, she had involved herself in a not too well thought out rebound relationship.

All I could think of after having met him that one time at the apartment was *Christ, Maria…I hope you know what the fuck you're getting into*. It was her life, and one which I was in the process of happily becoming uninvolved in. There would certainly be no advice forthcoming from me.

The salon had a new manager, Andrew, who was from within the salon staff itself and had been with the company for about two years. He had previously owned his own salon down in Maryland, and the company felt safe in appointing him to become the manager, because of his maturity and experience. He had also been recommended for the position by Donny, our new Regional Manager.

More times than not, Andrew and I did not see eye to eye and had a somewhat adversarial relationship, even when he was just a salon staff member. We simply did not get along prior to his being named salon manager, let alone after. On my part, I simply wanted a bit of respect for the role that I had played in the company over a period of the past nine or ten years, and he, egotistical prick that he was, just simply refused to give it to me. After he had been made salon manager, I kept mostly to myself, focused on my clientele, and concentrated on being the new *kinder, gentler me.*

There eventually came a point where he finally acquiesced himself to simply letting me do my own thing, and frankly, I don't think he wanted to have any type of confrontation any more than I did. He had been tasked with running the largest and most successful salon in the chain and had his own priorities to deal with, so we both just usually tried to avoid each other, and were, for the most part, generally cordial and business-like toward one another on a daily basis.

There was also no doubt in my mind that he was surely aware of the fact that I had friends in high places within corporate management and administration, and in that regard, he knew that I was simply not to be fucked with. If push came to shove, I could have had his head on a platter in a heartbeat, and he damn well knew it.

Tuesday morning before I started for the day, Donny called me to discuss the possibility of doing a seminar for two of our New Jersey salons. We talked briefly, and when I asked him for potential dates, he said he would get back to me. In passing, he mentioned that he had heard some disturbing rumblings from the corporate office. When I asked him what the nature of it was, he said that it was nothing for me to be concerned with right now, and not to worry about it. He would keep me informed if it turned out to be something of substance.

When I questioned him a bit more, he reiterated, and changed the subject, asking me how my divorce was coming along. I let it go and didn't pursue anything further. After all, what could possibly be going wrong at the corporate office? As far as I was aware, everything with the company was tip-top, everything was on a roll, and in all probability, it had to do with nothing more than a shakeup in some element of the hierarchy, which on any corporate level is to be expected.

A little after 1 P.M. I was just getting ready to leave the salon for a late lunch when Diane, our receptionist, told me I had another phone call. As I was in close proximity to the salon office at the rear of the salon, I retreated there to take the call in private, thinking it might be someone from corporate.

I was stunned to hear the voice of Rita, my former lover with whom I had such a tempestuous affair not all that long ago. I had not seen her in over 2 years.

Perhaps it was just me, the way that I was, and all that was ingrained in me, but from the moment I heard her voice on the other end of the phone, I almost immediately, in a flash of just a few seconds, relived every sexual tryst that I had with her. It was as though in talking to her, I could actually feel her...*feel how my cock had once felt inside her*...just from speaking with her on the phone.

She asked if I would cut her hair, apologized for not going through the receptionist, and said that she simply wanted to speak personally with me to book an appointment. *"It's been a long time, maybe we could go for coffee then. My hair is fucked up, and I haven't had a good cut... or anything else... since you."* It was cryptic, but I knew exactly what she meant.

I was truly stunned to hear from her, and my mind was going in a million different directions. *Christ, I needed her like a fucking hole in the head.* I was a new person now, or so I liked to *convince* myself of, and let there be no doubt that having been so pre-occupied with my getting together with Meeka in a few days, I simply did not know if at this point in time I wanted to burn the candle at both ends again. The fact of the matter is that there would be no one nighter with Rita...it was the way that she was. She would not rest until she had you hooked, thus I had to be cautious, but that being said, sometimes weakness will prevail over caution.

I leaned my head up against the office wall as I was conversing with her, giving my forehead several light taps, as if to somehow bang some sense into my head and gather the strength to say no, but the fact of the matter is that I was indeed weak, and I caved in to her request.

I agreed to see her as a client once again, and told her to come in at 8 P.M. I would stay a bit later to do her hair.

As I proceeded through my roster of booked clients during the day, all I could think of to myself was *Good Lord, what in fuck's name am I getting myself into with her again?...I had better really think this thing out while I still have time...I should have just told her, no.*

In addition, Maria called almost immediately after I had hung up with Rita and wanted to know if I was available for a meeting with our realtor that night, to discuss offers we had received on the house. I told her it would have to wait, that I was booked solid, and, lying to her of course, said that I was invited to a client's house for a late dinner that night. I told her I would either call her when I got home if it wasn't too late, or perhaps call the next morning. She had been off from work at the salon that day and being as unreasonable as she could be at times, flew off the handle, and told me what an uncaring bastard I was, that I didn't give a shit about getting this all wrapped up, and that it was of primary importance to us both to finally get things over with. With that, she hung up on me.

I was in no mood. As sexual of a person as I had always been, I had nonetheless always been the type that simply *could not perform* or *function*, when I had something weighing heavy on my mind; in this case, getting my balls busted by a soon to be ex-wife. Arguing with her, when she was in that mood, could deflate an erection, or the potential of one, faster than you could imagine. Going under the assumption that there was even a *remote possibility* that I was going to fuck Rita again that night, and given the fact that she could be so exhausting and demanding sexually, the last thing I needed was having to contend with any bullshit from Maria to max out my stress level beyond what it was.

I was once again going through a mental tug of war as I had at times put myself through previously. I truly thought that by this time I was finally on a path to redemption, so I didn't need any of this on my plate with either Maria or Rita. It was indeed tempting though, simply because Rita was *such a great fuck*. I composed myself even though I was to the greater degree conflicted, and to some degree, actually pissed off at myself for agreeing to see Rita again. *Where the hell was my head at, for Christ's sake?*

The more that I thought about it though, the more I began to rationalize that seeing Rita once again, and possibly taking her back as a steady client, *did not mean that I had to fuck her.* I could just as easily act somewhat aloof but pleasant when she came in, and avoid anything else that might ensue. I simply didn't know what I was going to do, and thought that I would just let the situation play itself out when she came in.

She arrived for her appointment about 10 minutes early that night, shortly before 8 P.M. As it was a somewhat warm June evening, she had on a petite mini sun dress baring her golden brown tanned skin in just the right places, as well as a dressy pair of sandals that showed off her gorgeous little freshly pedicured feet, done with hot red nail polish on the toes.

In terms of being a seductress, Rita was polished…one of the best. This was especially so when she was going after *someone* that she wanted. If anything, she was a master at that which she did, and I knew that from before. If she intended to snare me once again, she had certainly not forgotten the manner in which she could yank *my chains.*

Rita knew what a sucker I was for a beautiful pair of feet, she knew how and when to show just enough skin, and most of all, she knew how to look directly at me with those incredible eyes of hers. In all probability, or so I surmised, she probably didn't have any underwear on that night either; her trademark, so to speak, that she had teased me with so many times before…*beyond provoking me.*

She knew just how to weaken a male, and knew damn good and well that would be exactly the trap that I was capable of falling into, had she caught me at the right time.

Kissing me on my cheek and asking me how I was, I could distinctly hear her inhale slightly, trying to take in the scent of my skin. *"I knew it, Jovan Musk, right?"* I nodded my head, as I looked her directly in the eyes. She just shook her head back and forth and said, *"God damn, you always smelled so good. I thought you used to wear it just for me, but I guess not."* She then leaned up and softly whispered in my ear, making sure that no one was close by, *"I even liked the way your dick smelled."* I just shook my head slowly, and smiled back at her mischievously, showing just a bit of humorous distain at her comment and said, *"Well...I see you haven't changed."*

Getting right down to it, I immediately put myself in motion with all the particulars of getting on with her haircut; getting a cape on her, and leading her back to the shampoo area at the rear of the salon. We were by ourselves and as I was shampooing her and manipulating through the slippery suds, she was letting out soft moans, at one point saying, *"Oh, God, I missed those hands."*

As we conversed, I told her of my pending divorce, my travels to New York almost every weekend, and that I was no longer as deeply involved in company education, thus not traveling as much I had been previously. As it was later in the night, the salon was for the most part empty except for Diane the receptionist, who was up front preparing things for the next day before she left. Our conversation continued as I led her up to my chair and I asked her what she had been up to. Surprisingly, she said she was in a relationship with a lawyer from one of the larger law firms in Philadelphia.

Rita was always one to be candid. *"He's ok I guess, he's a good guy and has lots of money, but he's not ringing any bells yet."* She was undoubtedly referring to her lack of ability to have an orgasm with him. Anyone else would have taken it at face value, but I knew *exactly* what she meant...I had been there before with her. Looking up, she then said, *"He's not you."*

I could feel the expectation level she had for the night, but at that point, if she was looking for a response from me, she was not going to get it. I was starting to realize that this whole thing was indeed a ruse...a trap. She was taking for granted that all she had to do was come into the salon, flash some skin, and speak to me in that seductive way that only she could, and that I would simply throw the towel in and start to see her again. Perhaps if it was any other set of circumstances, and I did not have a possible involvement with Meeka weighing so heavily on my mind, I would have indeed fell back into the trap and into my old ways again.

I mustered enough inner strength to stay silent. Had I answered her and steered the conversation in exactly the direction that I wanted, something that I was an absolute master at, it would have set the course for the rest of the night, and in all probability in less than an hour I could have been fucking her silly at the apartment, but I prevailed, and said nothing.

By the time I had finished cutting her hair, we were the last two in the salon. Diane had left for the evening, Andrew had left for the day a few hours earlier, and I was obviously tasked with closing up the salon.

As I led her to the front, she asked what I was doing for the rest of the night but by then I was now truly at the point where I was getting pissed off at what I knew she presumed, and could plainly see where she was trying to go with the whole thing. I would not be hers on a whim.

With that, I told her that I had to get together with Maria to discuss offers on the house and that we were under time constraints. Of course, in saying that, it was nothing more than allowing myself a quick exit from the conversation, and perhaps she even knew that I was lying. By that time, all I wanted to do was get home, call Meeka to firm things up for the weekend, and settle in for the night. It had been a busy day, and I was in no mood for her games. Mentally, I had prevailed.

I guess I *had* changed. Just a few years earlier, there would have been no such thing as *me* being *too tired* or *too conflicted* to fuck *anyone*. She asked if I would call her, and I simply said that I just did not know if or when, and that I had a lot going on.

Frustrated by her lack of ability to succeed, she then lit a cigarette, and smiled as she looked up at me. Slowly shaking her head back and forth in what was obviously an appearance of frustration, she caressed the side of my face with her hand and said, *"You always made me crazy."*

Perhaps her intention was to just make that one last point with the physical touch of her hand on my face that would communicate to me that in the two years or so that had gone by since our affair, she had finally come to a realization….a realization that what she previously had with me really was something more than just sex, and that perhaps during our past time together she did indeed love me, but just didn't allow it to come to the surface. Perhaps our sexual chemistry and the manner in which she simply *loved the way that I fucked her,* had completely overshadowed any feelings that she had for me at the time.

Taking in a slight breath, she kissed me on the cheek and said, *"Can't blame a girl for tryin', huh?* With that, she walked out of the salon, blowing me one more kiss with her hand as she exited, and was gone. I never saw her again.

After Rita left, I closed the salon up for the night and hurriedly made my way back to my apartment. It was well past 9 P.M. I still had to call Maria up and get the specifics concerning the offers we had on the house, and then try and get ahold of Meeka at either the gallery or her apartment.

Arriving home, I called Maria first, just as she was apparently getting ready to leave with her boyfriend Andre, for the night. She was surprisingly calm compared to her demeanor a few hours earlier when she had called me at the salon to inform me of the offers on the house, and ended up hanging up the phone on me.

After discussing things, we decided to accept one of the offers that came in at full asking price. In the morning I would call Gloria, our real estate agent to tell her, in addition to calling Tom, my business lawyer, and have him set forth a closing date for the purchase. It was almost over.

Of course, Maria had to get one last verbal jab in and asked me if I was by myself that night, in which case I sensed her sarcasm and meaning. She was obviously getting laid by that cocky Russian fucker whom I despised. I simply told her to go fuck herself and hung up. I had many more important things to do.

I then called Meeka at the gallery in SoHo, and was told that I had missed her by a good 20 minutes. I waited another ten minutes or so before trying to call her apartment, giving her a little more time to get home, and hoping that she had not gone out for the night after leaving work. In the meantime, I poured a glass of wine for myself, and then went into the bedroom and retrieved a joint that I had in my jewelry box that had to be at least 2 months old. I was hoping that it was still fresh.

Wine always loosened me up and made me a bit more *ethereal* in both my thinking and the way that I talked; perhaps a little more worldly and philosophical sounding.

Of course with the added kick of a little bit of weed, I would be precisely in the mood that I needed to be in to speak to Meeka. For me, there was always something about the combination of being high and drinking just the right amount of wine that also made me a bit more *ballsy*. Perhaps it made me a little more mysterious sounding as well, and conveyed a side of me that I hoped she would see as we talked.

In my mind I wanted her to be as anticipative as I was about the coming weekend, even though I was merely surmising about her intentions, thus if I said the right things, and *pushed the right buttons*, I might further stir her curiosity in me. Dialing the phone, it began to ring.

It only rang 3 times, but with the anticipation that I had, it might as well have rung 20 times and have been an almost endless wait before hearing her voice on the other end. She answered the phone, and didn't even say hello. *"You called; I knew it was you."* I was stunned. This was 1983...there was no caller ID. *"My God, how did you know? I can't believe,"* ...I stumbled for words, and as I did, she began to laugh, *"Ahh, now I have a secret."*

She was obviously amused by the way that she had confounded me and was making a jesting reference to that very first question she had initially asked me at the café just a few short days ago about *me* having some kind of a secret.

"So, you are coming in, yes?" I loved her accent. I could listen to her all day and was getting a major erection just hearing her talk. *"Yes, I'm coming in Meeka; I told you that I would call to confirm."* There was a few seconds of silence on the other end of the phone, and then she said to me *"Listen...no drink, no alcohol on the day before, ok? I need your body to be pure; yoga is pure and that will make things better. I want you to experience, ok?...the right way."*

I asked her where we should meet and she gave me her apartment address in SoHo on Prince Street. *"I want to show you the rest of my work too...the other things I do. Are you excited?"* I told her I was, and that I could not wait. *"What are you excited about? Is it the yoga, me, or my work?"*

It was as if she was laying a bit of a mischievous verbal trap for me, but in doing so, it was not malicious, it was without question a combination of teasing, of curiosity, and of simply acting like women act when they are testing you and perhaps searching the inside of you a bit. I answered, "*Everything, of course, and that includes cutting your hair*". With a girlish giggle, she said, *"Ok, we shall see, we shall see."* She then said, *"I heard you are very good at what you do. I saw Louis again, he tell me"*. With that, she said rather teasingly, *"and so am I"*.

With that, I was now incredibly curious. We agreed to meet at 10 A.M. Saturday morning, and as we ended the conversation, said good night. As I hung up the phone, I could only lean back, almost in a daze.

She had me. Maybe it was the wine, or maybe it was the weed; I don't know. Surely though, it was because of her, and the effect that she had on me.

Chapter Thirteen
Tantra

Saturday morning I was up at 5 A.M. in order to get ready, throw a few things together for the weekend, and then take the 7:15 bus into Manhattan. I usually trekked into the city from the Norristown bus station, not far from where I lived. The ride was about 2 hours long.

The remaining week at the salon was an exceptionally busy one. That rest of the week had been a blur for the most part, given my preoccupation with going into the city and meeting up with Meeka.

I was also starting to forgive myself for *almost* caving in to Rita, and was quite pleased with what turned out to be a mental show of both strength and change on my part in that regard.

Wednesday I made all of my important phone calls, and took care of all pending business with the real estate agent as well as Tom, my lawyer. My priority was to be sure that there were no pressing needs or loose ends to be taken care of with either the sale of the house, or any of my obligations with the education department at the home office in Los Angles.

I told Maria I was going away for the weekend. Above and beyond everything, I just wanted to leave for Manhattan with a completely clear head, although admittedly, I was still thinking about the cryptic way that Donny had told me there might be something brewing at the corporate office. It bothered me, and had me wondering about what could possibly be going on, but I acquiesced myself to the fact that digging deeper would have to wait until I got back home from New York.

The bus arrived at the Port Authority at 9:25 that morning, so I had to hustle. I usually used the subway station one block north of the Port Authority on 8th Ave. The R train was the primary run down to SoHo. That station was always a bit crazy, since the R train was one of the primary runs from midtown, headed south to both Chelsea and SoHo. You could easily get slowed down during the peak of morning rush hour. Upon arriving, and seeing that I might be late for my rendezvous with Meeka, I practically ran through the Port Authority, with my over the shoulder bag flopping from side to side, as I hurried down the long corridor, which was its usual hustle of early morning activity. I made my way to the platform just in time to catch the next train as it was about to leave.

The 20-minute ride down to Prince Street felt agonizingly long. As usual, the subway car was hot and muggy, with the air conditioning barely working. In 1983, it was the *pre-Guilliani* days, and the New York subway system was nowhere near what it is today in terms of at least reasonable cleanliness…not that it's winning any prizes today by any stretch of the imagination, but in 1983, well before Rudolph Guilliani was mayor and cleaned things up, it was downright filthy, and at times, especially later in the evening after the commuting hours, you also had to have eyes in the back of your head.

In the summertime, the air conditioning on the trains was minimal at best. You would get on a train, and even after what was nothing more than a ten-minute ride, you felt like you needed a shower again.

After arriving at the Prince Street station, I made my way up the steps, elbow to elbow with the hundreds of morning commuters, and headed east to Meeka's apartment, carefully watching the addresses as I walked.

Her apartment was not too far away from the gallery that she worked at, and was just above a very upscale store that specialized in ultra contemporary Danish style furniture and housewares. You entered into the foyer through a side door.

I buzzed her apartment and she answered almost immediately on the intercom system. *"Good morning, who is this, please?"* Even on the intercom, her voice sounded sexy as hell. Feeling a bit giddy and mischievous, I answered. *"Well good morning, it's me. I'm here."* Laughing, she answered back, *"Ahh, mister hair man, you are late. Come up, I'm 2A, first door, left."*

As I climbed the stairs to the second floor, my mind began the usual self-check that I guess all men go through.

Had I merely thrown myself together in a rather cocky attitude of over self-confidence? Had I presumed that she was so attracted to me that no matter what I looked like she would literally rip my clothes off when I walked through the door? Or was this whole thing a fantasy on my part?

Perhaps I had read too much into this rendezvous from the very beginning, and from our first meeting at the café. Maybe all this was going to be was a gratis haircut for a new friend, an introduction to the physical art that she teaches, and nothing more than a private preview of the art that she hoped to establish her name with.

As my feet hit the top of the landing and my eyes went left, the door to her apartment opened almost simultaneously and she appeared, smiling and a bit out of breath, greeting me with both hands on her hips and sans makeup.

She was wearing a gray sleeveless athletic top, black spandex leggings, and was barefoot. *God, she had beautiful feet.* Even without the ruby red lipstick and full makeup that I had initially seen her wearing that very first time that we met, she was a vision. As she had done at the café a week previous when she said goodbye, she now greeted me in kind, kissing me hello on both cheeks, and asking how my ride into the city had gone that morning.

The apartment was spartan, with just a few pieces of furniture, a television set, table and chairs, and shelving throughout, on which there must have been close to 50 candles. The candles were obviously something she used to create mood, and perhaps to enhance her Avyeradic beliefs...something you would certainly expect from a practitioner of her caliber. It was apparent that she had done the apartment in such a way so that at times, when circumstances warranted it, it was a sacred place.

I said nothing as I let my eyes scan a full 360 degree view of what was obviously a typical New York City one-room loft with bathroom, where you simply make what you can out of it, and somehow decide which space is for sleeping, which space is for eating, and last but not least, where do you put a couch and TV.

There were two large mats in the center of the hardwood floor. She explained to me that this was where she practiced her yoga, and at times when not at the spa, where she taught private clients.

The walls were resplendent with meticulous photo groupings, all in oversized black frames; not just the erotic nudes she had shown me from her portfolio, but also quite a few photos that focused on the everyday people of New York. I marveled at the diversity. There were pictures of walkers, young rebels, the homeless, and a few architectural pictures of New York's magnificent buildings, photographed in such a way so as to show off both their geometry and period influence. She knew her craft, and told a story with each shot, using just the right lighting, a hint of background blur, and a knowledge of distance.

"*My work, do you like?*" In asking the question, she for the first time was not exhibiting the same cocky attitude that she had exhibited at the café, but rather it was truly rhetorical. *She wanted me to like them.* She was no longer looking for praise, but rather, was truly looking for self-assurance, given to her by someone else.

I questioned certain pictures, asking where they were taken, what the circumstances were, and what her inspiration was.

As she explained her work, I commented on each photo in a way that showed her not just my approval, but also my working knowledge of both color and balance, the by-product of my being a highly trained method haircutter, with a number of disciplines under my belt. That training taught me to create shapes out of a malleable fiber that in turn, had to be accented in just the right way with hair color, and then photographed to make anyone, in particular my peers in the trade, look at the finished product, think, analyze, converse among themselves, and decide on the artistic prowess of.

She was undoubtedly gratified, but also, she could tell that I was not merely telling her the answers she wanted to hear; rather, I was a kindred spirit, a fellow artist that perhaps she could collaborate with…maybe even spend the rest of her life with, if indeed the circumstances were right. *"I think you like, yes? I can tell, you are sincere."*

Turning to me slowly and with her imperfect English, she said *"the other day at LaMond, you say I have good eye. I think you have good eye too. You understand my work".* I didn't know quite what to say, and there was a moment of awkward silence. I had obviously passed the *second test* with her…the first test having been a week previous at the café during our first meeting, thus resulting with her inviting me to come in to the city to cut her hair…as well as for anything else that she have planned.

"So, are you ready to begin? I think that perhaps we can start."

She paused for a moment, and turned to light a few more candles. I could only stare at the rear view of her beautiful body, the way that the tight spandex hugged every perfect curve, and the way that it was almost artfully silhouetted in the sunlight coming through the window. *"We will relax after, with some wine, then haircut, yes? I think you know exactly what you want to do to me."*

She was obviously referring to how I was going to cut her hair, but for a brief moment, I showed a bit of hesitation, and perhaps shock, thinking that she was referring to something sexual.

She turned and moved closer to me, wrapping her arms around my neck, leaned up, and kissed me. I was caught off guard, completely not expecting it...I was in fact, stunned, and completely not expecting her to be so aggressive.

It was at that point that I knew that in our first meeting at the café, and in that brief period of time that it had lasted, that something had indeed happened. On my part, it might have been physical obsession, combined with a bit of wonderment and a bit of lust...but with her, there was something else more profound.

Somehow, some way, she apparently had an immediate attraction to me, and perhaps a belief that maybe...just maybe, she had found her kindred soul, wanting to totally explore that possibility, least it escapes her and cause future regret.

She whispered almost inaudibly in my ear as though there were other people in the apartment and she wanted no one to hear...*"I need to ask you this, and I want you just listen...please...I need to know why you are here...I need to know if you like me, because I like you, and I have feeling...a feeling about you; but If you are here to just fuck me and leave, you are mistaken. I do not fuck; I make love, and I do not make love unless I feel love in return; but first, you must learn about me, and I must learn about you, and see if this can work...see if my feeling about you is right. This is something we must do, and if you can not, then you must leave now."*

I slowly began to shake my head back and forth in a gesture that said *no...no, I was not leaving, and yes, I wanted to be there with her...right then, right there, in that place and at that time...*and that my intentions were nothing less than being the same as hers. I began to feel like I was in a *dream world*. She was taking control of me in a manner such as I had never experienced before. It was happening fast, and it was not what I expected.

I told her how I felt. I told her how beautiful I thought she was, and I told her that from the very first time that I saw her at the café, it was as though I had been struck by lightning. I was saying things to her that I never thought I would say to any woman. It was more than lust on my part; I was becoming infatuated with her, and letting her take the lead.

For the first time in my adult life as a male who had slept with so many women before, and who was so sexually experienced, I felt a bit out of my realm. I was used to being both the aggressor as well as the teacher, and it appeared that there was every possibility that I was now going to find myself playing the role of being *the student*. She smiled at me and kissed me again, this time slowly moving up my cheek and nibbling at my ear lobe in a teasing manner that made me want to simply explode.

"Come then...for all that we will do, you must cleanse first, and you did not wear loose clothing. I forgot to tell you, but no matter, you will not need them; we will both be naked, that is my way. You must begin to think of the body as sacred."

Leading me to the bathroom, she instructed me to shower, and to take my time in doing so, as it would relax and prepare me. After the shower, I was to go back to the living area where the mats were.

After an exceptionally relaxing hot shower of at least 15 minutes, I stepped out of the bathroom and into the main room as I was drying off with a lavender scented towel. She had placed flowers and candles around the large mats that were on the floor and she was naked; her back to me as she lit the candles and then stood to prepare incense that was on a table close by. Her body was beautiful; slim and incredibly toned, from that which she had obviously been practicing for so very long.

Soft Indian music, barely audible, played in the background and I sensed the fragrance of both the burning incense as well as what I later found out to be exotic oils that were warming and permeating the air.

As she turned and I approached her, she gently shook her head and said *"Do not touch me; it must wait. First, you must learn about yourself and your body, and then, learn about my body, too."*

She said that we would begin with simple deep breathing, and asked that I look directly at her, as she too looked directly at me. We started with her showing me a mutual breathing pattern, and as we did so, we established the same rhythm. Within no time, I was feeling relaxed and somewhat euphoric, which I attributed to the atmosphere she had created as well as the entire focus on breathing.

She then told me to lay on my side, and she too then laid on her side facing me. In that position, we repeated the breathing. After a few moments, we stood back up, facing each other and continuing to breath. She then said, *"Look at me, and continue; look at my body."* She smiled, and as I looked directly into her eyes, it was as though we were physically touching each other. As per her instructions, I then let my eyes take in the entirety of her body from top to bottom. It was then, that I came to the realization that she was indeed, the most beautiful woman I had ever seen.

Taking both of my hands in hers, she guided me through a series of stretching exercises, first standing, then kneeling, and then with the both of us laying on the floor. After what was close to 30 minutes of teaching me to breathe, stretch, flex my body, and then relax, she finally let me touch her, and she, in turn, touched me. If this was foreplay, then it was something I had never done before...something almost cosmic and otherworldly.

We were making circular tracing movements on each other, individually taking turns moving from the forehead, then slowly down the sides of the face, and ultimately moving down the entire body, stopping and focusing on those areas that would inevitably cause arousal. She began schooling me in the seven chakras of touch, physically showing me each one, and then verbally explaining the specifics of what they were individually meant to achieve.

The entire morning and the learning experience that ensued was a journey. It involved all of the senses; touch, feel, sight, sound, and smell. I did not want it to end. To some degree, it was reminiscent of the mellow highs that I had achieved in the past when I experimented with certain moderate drugs of choice, but yet it was all done through vision, touch, feel, and proper breathing.

I learned about *my* body, and she taught me about *hers*...how to *read* her, how to give her pleasure in a specific way that was unique to just her and her individual desires and needs. She taught me about a world I had not known existed. I learned about *Shiva (masculine energy)* and *Shakti (feminine energy)*, and that in merging the two you become one. I also learned that nothing must be taken for granted, and that in a developing relationship there must be a mutual respect for each other. It must always start with the physical respect and knowledge of your partner's body, and thus anticipating each other's responses on an intimate level, before there is sex. Only then, could it develop into the highest of emotional bonds...*love.*

Ultimately, we did indeed make love, and then become *one*. I had never felt such mental awareness in having sex. I was conscious of everything. Not just in the way that she felt physically with my cock inside her, but rather what it conveyed in emotional feeling as well. The physical part of sex, for me, had previously always been separate from the emotional, if indeed there ever was anything emotional with whomever I was with at the time.

Now, for the first time, it was acting in a harmony that I had never felt before. With Meeka, it had become one thing; one entity.

Later that afternoon, I cut her hair. As I did so, she somehow brought out a passion in me for my art that I had not known or felt in quite some time. We were both naked as I cut her hair, and as I carved through the beautiful black fiber, soft wisps of the shorn hair fell on her body, and she gently brushed them from her breasts and perfectly tight stomach down to the floor. I felt as though I was Michelangelo putting the finishing touches on the Venus De Milo.

After I finished cutting her hair, we showered together, and once more made love. Her orgasms were intense. Although she was not loud, she quietly moaned and panted. I felt her shudder and lightly shake, as she held on to me tighter with each of my thrusts, her legs wrapped tightly around my waist and back. When we were done, I knew what we had both achieved, both mentally and physically. We simply just laid there, my cock still inside her, and still hard.

Even though we both came, because I was still inside her, I could still feel her pulsing rhythmically and internally holding on to my cock like a vice. We eventually fell asleep, but it was not from exhaustion; it was from the splendor of it all that inevitably brings on such a complete tranquility. I did not go home Saturday evening as planned, and spent the night.

By late Sunday, it was now time for me to leave. I felt as though we had been together for years, and in so many ways, I felt like I was an entirely different person. What had she done to me? Despite all of my previous efforts to change, failing each time, it finally took *her* to bring the change in me that I had long yearned for.

This was beyond that which I had experienced with all of my past relationships. It was beyond the meaningless affairs that I had with Rita, or Adrianna, or any of the other women I had slept with. None of the others were capable of bringing to the surface any of the elements that would give me emotional peace, and in turn, they left me empty emotionally, even though I had been sexually fulfilled with them.

As I prepared to go home to Philadelphia, Meeka made me promise that I would call her during the week, and that I would come back into Manhattan the following weekend. She wanted to be with me, and she told me so.

As I went down the steps that led from her apartment, she stood at the top of the stairs, and I kept turning to look back as I descended. I didn't want to forget the vision. I didn't want to forget that which we had forged in a mere 48 hours.

Making my way to the Port Authority and boarding the bus back to King of Prussia, I was certain of two things; I knew that my life was about to change because of her, and I also knew that I had fallen head over heels in love.

Chapter Fourteen
Barbarians At The Gate

I returned to King of Prussia and finally got back to my apartment close to 11 Sunday night. I was giddy with the excitement of my weekend in New York with Meeka, and the anticipation of now finally developing what may well become the most important relationship of my life. I now wanted finality to the divorce, and wanted it to happen in the most expedient way possible.

I was almost dizzy reliving all that had happened, and in my mind, was reliving the events *as they had happened.* I felt like I was the ancient man who might have first discovered fire, only in this case, what I discovered was a true peace and degree of happiness in myself that I did not know existed before. I also knew that big decisions about my life would have to come forth, depending on any number of events that would possibly transpire.

I had previously toyed with the idea of leaving the company after voluntarily stepping down, and out of my full time roles in education and management. Now that I had met Meeka, I wondered if I should indeed move to New York City, and for that matter, if I did, could I then succeed there in my career. New York was a city that could eat you up and spit you out in a heartbeat. Moving there would be not just be a major event for me, but a life test as well.

I poured a glass of wine for myself, and sat in relative silence. I began to both think about and prioritize the steps of what it would take to egress from my life as it was, take my relationship with Meeka to the next level, and start over again in a new city. I also wondered if all that was possibly brewing within the company might then create a situation that would in some way expedite my decision-making.

Finishing my drink, I fell asleep on the couch and slept straight through until just past 9 A.M. the next morning. Monday I was off from work. I had laundry and errands to do, and would call Donny some time before noon. I would simply insist that he let me in on exactly what might be going on, if indeed there was anything at all. I was a senior employee with tenure. The way that I looked at it, anything that happened at the corporate office may well have some type of long-term affect on my career, therefore *I needed to know,* in order to be able to plan the rest of my life. Perhaps if I had not met Meeka, I would not have been so focused on such an expeditious time frame. I had now made up my mind that Meeka would indeed be part of any new life, and that I would pursue her. There was every possibility that I had found the one person that I would be paired with for the rest of my days.

I put a call into Donny's office after running around all morning and accomplishing most of my errands. He was apparently out on the road, so I left a message for him to call me back. I made up my mind that if I had not heard from him by Monday night, I would call again on Tuesday, and with that, I was now starting to feel quite a bit of anxiety…there was so much to think about and decide on.

Later that night, I called Meeka, and we picked up exactly where we had left off. Even though it had only been 24 hours since we saw each other, we expressed how much we already missed each other, and what a wonderful weekend it had been. It was as though I was still at the apartment, and as we spoke, I visualized her with every word that came out of her mouth. We talked for over an hour, and spoke of all the things we would do the following weekend…going to the park, going out for dinner, and of course, making love.

Tuesday morning I returned to the salon a bit later than usual, as I still had remaining errands to take care of before making my way to the mall to start work. Stopping for coffee along the way, I bumped into Charlene, my former *hump from the mall*, and she happened to be with her girlfriend, Uma.

I squirmed at seeing them sitting together at one of the front tables, which was visible from the large window that bordered the sidewalk on the corner of where the coffee shop was located.

I had at one time or another fucked the both of them, and in seeing them together, I was leery that any approach and subsequent direct conversation might indeed be awkward.

I had every reason to believe that Charlene *didn't know* that Uma and I had secretly been together on several occasions, but honestly, I could not be sure. For all I knew, Charlene may have been aware, and could give a shit less, or, maybe at some point in their mutual discussion of me, they simply compared notes.

Uma was cute and had a great body, but there was no way that I could have ever had a relationship with her. She was one of the few women I was ever with that was into anal sex in a major way; she in fact, loved it, and had incredible orgasms as a result. But with her, it was all about pure lust, and at times was emotionless and uncaring, to some degree almost emotionally greedy. The way that I looked at it though, those few times that I was with her were nothing more than a series of one night stands, and we did nothing less than use each other for mutual gratification. I was a notch on her belt, and she was a notch on mine. I didn't really have an attraction to her in any way. She was nothing more than an exceptional fuck in bed, who embellished herself and any man she was with, with one of the greatest of sexual pleasures.

I entered the coffee shop, and since Charlene had already seen me approaching through the front window, she waved me over.

"Where the fuck have you been? I haven't seen you out in months". I gave myself a reason to get out of the conversation quickly by telling her that I was running late and couldn't talk long, but also tried to provide a quick answer. I told her that I had been going into Manhattan quite a bit on *'company business'*. Of course, that was not true, but I just wanted to gracefully exit from the conversation as quickly as I could, and get on my way.

Uma just looked down after saying a brief but pleasant hello, feigning that she only knew me casually, but in doing so, confirming my thoughts. Charlene apparently *did not know* that Uma and I had been together. Even girlfriends apparently have their secrets.

"Call me, you prick; I miss you." Leaving the conversation on a pleasant note, I smiled and simply said, *"Ok Char, maybe next week if I'm around; been a while, I know, but I've just been swamped."*

I was always very good at ending conversations and making an amicable exit, and in doing so, saying only that which I had to, in order to end things and move on.

I got to the mall close to 9:45, which for me, was late. Andrew's wary eye caught me coming in, as we had crossed paths at the salon entrance just as he was running out. I presumed that he was perhaps headed to the bank to make the previous day's deposit, but we didn't speak. My first client was waiting for me, and I had to stay on time. I hated running late and rushing my work. I glanced at the appointment book upon coming in, and saw that I was booked solid with clients for or the entire day.

I was five minutes into my first client of the morning, shortly after 10 A.M., when Diane the receptionist came over to tell me that there was a phone call for me from Don. He was finally returning my call.

With that, she said, "*He said to tell you that it's urgent.*" I excused myself apologetically from my client, explaining the circumstances of the call, and told her that I would just be a few minutes. I then made my way back to the privacy of the salon office.

As I picked up the phone and asked Donny what was going on, I could tell within a second of first hearing the quivering manner of his voice, that whatever it was, it wasn't good. "*Hey man, I have some very bad news. I just got off of the phone with Ron at the office; Mr. Schwartzman is stepping down and the company is being sold.*"

I said nothing and listened in stunned silence, waiting for more, and with my first thoughts then being *are you fucking kidding me?* I felt like I had been hit with a sledgehammer.

Donny apologized for having been a bit standoffish with me a few days earlier and explained that based on the limited and unconfirmed information that he had when we spoke previously, it truly was nothing more than rumor and speculation at the time.

Howard L. Schwartzman the 3rd had been the respected CEO of the company since its initial concept. He was also the primary individual responsible for gathering much of the initial financial investment that would catapult the company from having been a small local chain of several West Coast based salons, into its current status of having corporate locations and franchises in almost every state.

Don then went on to explain the details of what had transpired, based on what he had been told up to that point. I found myself getting numb with almost every word that came out of his mouth. The situation had apparently been brewing for some time.

Apparently, Schwartzman's health had been going down hill. He was in the early stages of an aggressive form of MS and he had been keeping it a secret from the board of directors. In addition, the company finances were dipping into the red from what was, in essence, unchecked expansion that relied on bank credit, as well as the company's good name and growth posture for the last several years. Incoming revenues were simply not keeping up with debt, and some way, some how, he was able to hide it from the board.

He also was apparently suffering from early onset Alzheimer's disease, as Donny alluded to by noting that when he was present at corporate meetings that Schwartzman was overseeing, Schwartzman would at times appear distant, and on a few occasions repeated himself on matters, forgetting that they were already discussed; that in itself, was enough to raise red flags to those who had also been present at the meetings. They just presumed that it was fatigue, as well as the heavy workload that came with the responsibility of the position.

At some point, Schwartzman had to inform the board of the situation after they demanded to know what was causing the sea of red ink. A no-confidence vote was cast, and Schwartzman was asked to resign. Prior to any search for a replacement for the position, the situation was assessed and deemed unsalvageable. A decision was made to sell the company. This occurred over a period of several weeks and subsequent clandestine board meetings. An offer was on the table from an independent conglomerate of investors from both Canada and Europe. That conglomerate had substantial holdings within the salon industry globally, not just in other mall based salon chains, but in product manufacturing as well. They were huge.

As stunned as I was, I could not help but think to myself that the board members, perhaps not all of them, and *certainly not Frederick*, whom I'm sure would have cast a dissenting vote to sell, had decided to take what might best be called a *golden parachute*.

After listening intently in silence, I finally said, *"Christ, Donny, what the hell are we going to do?"*

He said that we should just stay calm, that there simply wasn't enough information yet, and that we should not immediately assume that our careers were in jeopardy. With a new acquisition of the company, and thus with a cash infusion and financial rescue, it may well result in something better. For all we knew, the stock that we owned might even increase in value. We could only speculate on things at that point, as we conversed about the possibilities.

He promised to keep me abreast of all that was happening on a daily basis. As I hung up the phone, regardless of his trying to placate the situation, I had every reason to believe that *it...our thing, our life, and everything that we had all mutually embellished ourselves to* for almost ten years was most likely over, as would be any upward career status for all of us who were considered to be key personnel within the company.

I returned to my client in stunned silence, and how I got through that haircut without fucking it up is beyond me.

I was overwhelmed. I couldn't think straight, but had to put on a good face. In addition, Donny had asked me to keep a lid on things until there was more information, and to not say anything that would panic the rest of the employees. Pending future developments, whatever they might be, an announcement of some sort would eventually be made. At the time, the situation was only 24 hours old, and many questions and considerations still had to be answered and taken into account.

About two hours after having spoken to Don, Andrew came back to the salon after having been gone most of the morning for what apparently was a doctor's appointment.

As I was in between client bookings, he asked me to come back to the office, and with a bit of an ashen face said to me *"Did you speak to Donny yet? You know what's going on, right?"*

Andrew had obviously been informed at some point earlier than I was, and was every bit as stunned. We just shook our heads and mutually consoled each other. Although we had not gotten along in the past it seemed as though he was now approaching me as a peer and confidante, saying, *"You know I can't believe this is happening now, just as I'm getting a leg up on this fucking place, and now all this bullshit has to happen."*

He asked me about my weekend travels to New York and the fact that I was going into the city so much. He also asked me rather directly if I had anything going on, or possibly pending there, in regards to a job. I had no reason to hide anything. I simply told him that with my divorce from Maria now being almost complete, and with the house now having been sold, I didn't know what I would do, especially in lieu of today's events.

I then told him about Meeka, and he asked if I would be moving there. *"Christ, Andrew, I don't know, I really don't. With all this shit today, and trying to wrap up this damn divorce, I really have no idea. Maybe at some point I will, depending on what goes on."*

I was shocked to hear him offer that he did not blame me if I did move, and that he too had his family, finances, and future career to be concerned with as well. Andrew was a relative newbie to the company, with less than three years under his belt, compared to my ten-year tenure.

He was trying to be every bit as optimistic as Don was, and echoed the rationale that no one at this point should presume the worst....that big companies can offer big futures and that our best bet was to just *"go along for the ride"* for the time being, and see what happens.

Andrew had always been very much pro company. In light of the circumstances of my being so upfront with him and indicating that I would even consider making a move in the middle of all this chaos, he could have easily been a real prick about things, and then told just the right people above me about any thoughts that I had to possibly leave during such a critical time. Although that could have made things a bit heated for me, it probably wouldn't have mattered much. I certainly would not have gotten fired; I would have just had my *balls busted in a major way*, by both Frederick and Ron. Undoubtedly, they both would have done everything in their power to talk me out of it. It would have been as if I was a traitor abandoning ship at the worst possible time.

I returned to the apartment that night after what fared out to be one of the longest and most excruciating days since I had started with the company. Bad news has a way of doing that to you.

I got out of my clothes, smoked a joint that had been given to me by one of the girls at the salon earlier in the day, and poured some wine.

In my call to Meeka the previous night, she told me that she would be working later nights for the entire week. She and the rest of the staff were preparing hangings for a very important gallery show, and in all probability, she would not be home until some time past 11 each night. Both the wine and the weed gave me a chance to unwind, and think about what my conversation would be with her.

Shortly after 11, I called Meeka's apartment and she answered the phone promptly, saying that she had actually arrived home a bit earlier than anticipated, as they had extra help that evening, and she was able to make a quick exit from the gallery. She immediately sensed a difference in the tone of my voice, and after asking me if anything was wrong, listened patiently in quiet silence as I told her in detail about the day's events, as well as the uncertainty it could cause with both the company and my future career. She was sympathetic, but also seized the moment.

"Come...come to New York. Come and live here, there is so much here, and now there is me. You will do well here because you are such an artist with what you do." She then went on to tell me how much she loved her haircut, and that with all of the people that she knew in the arts, I would have an almost instantaneous clientele, just by her word of mouth, and circle of influential friends.

I told her that the possibility of making a move had been on my mind for quite some time, even prior to meeting her, and that although I certainly had cause to do so now, I would have to give the entire thing some thought. She understood that I had to ride this thing out, not just for my sake, but for the sake of those I had worked with for so long and was so close to. We were not the type to abandon each other, and leaving now would be nothing short of a *cop out*.

She was silent at first but then said, *"Sweet thing, you are, what is the word...stress?"* I laughingly corrected her. *"Yes, stressed, very stressed. But talking to you is making it better, believe me."*

We chatted a bit more, and after we hung up, I leaned back on the couch and smiled to myself. It was precisely the conversation that I needed; just talking to her brought a calmness to me, and relief from what was otherwise a horrible fucking day.

The days and weeks went on, and we saw each other every weekend. At times, we *fucked*; at times, *we made love*. Anyone who is experienced at *both* knows the difference. One is carnal, lustful, and perhaps *almost animalistic*. The other is gentle, soft, and filled with a giving of mutual feeling, of completely surrendering oneself, and of emotion coming from both the mind and the soul, as well as the heart.

She continued to teach me yoga as well as the whole scope of the tantric arts. In no time I knew just by sight, sound, and feel, *how and when* to approach her, *how* to touch her, and *where* to touch her. The more that we bonded both physically and mentally, it was becoming second nature to me.

On those long weekends in New York City, I was slowly leaving my life as it had been behind; everything, right back to the very beginning. For me, it was a purposeful self-purging. The many past memories were slowly being erased...the lousy factory jobs that I had before the start of my real career, the fact that I almost got trapped in a small town that would have completely buried my creative soul, and most of all, the 8 years that I had spent in an unhappy marriage. It was as though none of it had every existed, and that I was being completely reborn into a whole new life; as though God had decided to give me a new soul.

From that point on, we did everything together...*everything*. We went to Bryant Park regularly, went out to dinner, went to plays, and in the simplest of ways, we had fun.

The summer was very hot, and the undersized air conditioner that she had in her apartment barely cooled things off. We would buy two large containers of different flavored ice cream, and sit naked at her small dining table, spooning it to each other, trying to stay cool. As I would give her a *chocolate* kiss and try to meld it with the sweet *cherry vanilla* that was on her lips, we would laugh, and kiss, and laugh some more... *naked ice cream, cherry chocolate kisses*...it was the best part of the summer.

She introduced me to her friends and peers in the art world. Through her, I met people that I previously would have never even thought of meeting, let alone be in the same room with.

At one gathering in particular, Andy Warhol was there, as well as the new up and coming artist Jean Basquiat. Basquiat, admiring Meeka's haircut, commented on it as he passed by us.

I was floored. *Me*, talking with Basquiat; *Me*, at a gathering with Warhol. It was unbelievable.

Meeka and I were now recognized as a couple, we were in love, and we were inseparable. It was a glorious time.

In the morning upon awakening, the first words out of both our mouths would be those of expressing how much we loved each other. There was one morning in particular that I will never forget, and which defines just how quickly two people who are so right for each other can fall in love.

After having awakened in a face to face embrace, we looked at each other without uttering a word. Our eyes were locked for what had to be at least a full five minutes of silence, just gazing at each other, and rendering soft kisses to each other's lips; the kind of kisses where you are barely making contact, but which communicate so much. She then said to me in a voice that was just above a whisper, *"I know I am only 25, and I have not been with many men, but you...where have you been all my life? You are a gift."* With that, a tear slowly made its way out of one of her eyes, and we kissed some more. It was a tear of joy; a tear of pure emotion, which as I saw softly fall down her cheek, caused me to know that indeed, it came from the heart.

We started every day with chanting, a bit of yoga, and preparing ourselves to take on New York and all that it could throw at you.

Each day was about positive attitude, about commitment, and about respect for the fact that with life being as short as it is, you cannot succeed nor have true happiness unless you are loved by someone who gives you strength, and mutually shares all of your emotions, convictions, and values. I would not give her up for anything, and I was faithful to her. For the very first time in my life, the thought of even looking at another woman never even entered my mind.

I did several more photo shoots with Louis, and he and I were now becoming recognized by the agencies. We started to get offers for substantial amounts of money to do magazine work, as well as from the modeling agencies for portfolio development. We also had a mutual understanding that no matter which of us had been approached for work, be it he or I, that he didn't work without me, and I didn't work without him. We were a team.

By August, the sale of the company was made public. The closing date and signing of the papers was scheduled to happen just after the beginning of the year, and things were slowly changing.

The employees had been made aware of the sale of the company in an optimistically worded letter that was sent to all. Ultimately, there was the beginning of a mass exodus of salon staff from a number of the salons. They were very obviously not in the mood to hang around or wait for a promised outcome. At the same time, many saw their opportunity to leave and then open their own salons prior to the final contract of sale being put in place. The reasoning was simple; in all probability, the non-compete agreements that all stylists had signed which prevented them from opening up a salon any closer than 10 miles from *any* of the then existing company salons, would in all probability not be enforced. For many, time was of the essence, as inevitably the new corporation would mandate that a new non-compete contract would have to be put in place for all employees.

The company simply had too much on its plate legally and otherwise. The disposition and litigation of things of that nature could be both costly and time-consuming, even for a company like ours, who prior to the buyout, did indeed have a working team of legal counsel. In better days, they would have pursued any geographic infraction of a former stylist's contract like rabid dogs, but not now; not with these circumstances.

I myself, as someone who was still very much considered to be a primary employee even though I had stepped out of management and education, as well as because of my overall tenure, had a non-compete agreement for 25 miles.

Every day was bringing new phone conversations and late night meetings among those of us who had been so closely knit and involved with each other in the company over the past 10 years.

It seemed that all of us had at one point or another heard *this, that, or the other*, about the new Canadian-Euro conglomerate that was buying us out. Some had talked to the higher-ups at the corporate office, and had been told rather optimistically that everything would be for the better. Regardless of that, the new mentality was fast becoming that of *every man for himself.*

We simply did not know if we wanted to be part of it, or for that matter, if the new company would want those of us who had been primary employees, to be part of the new structure. Obviously, they would be bringing in their own people to key positions, something that is not unusual in the corporate world.

Almost every day started out with a phone call to me from Don or from one of those individuals who could best be called *my inner circle*, informing me of who had resigned, or had simply quit, in anticipation of the takeover. It appeared at times that bodies were literally flying out the door. It also became evident as to exactly what was going on. As part of the buyout deal, the company had agreed on a buyout price, and part of the consideration for that price was for the company to *lighten the load*, before the sale was 100% consummated.

In order to make things viable in that particular case, the company would have to terminate those individuals in the corporate structure who were at the higher end of the salary spectrum, thereby making things fall in line with the offered purchase price. It also made complete sense, since the new corporate group would be bringing in their own people from Canada and Europe, in supposedly what they would want to be a smooth and non-intrusive way.

I found out sometime later in the aftermath of the entire thing, that one of the first execs to be terminated would have been Frederick. Subsequently, that move was indeed attempted, and failed miserably. It was completely without logic or forethought.

Frederick was the most respected and well-liked individual in the entire company. As head of education, he had always made it a point to be *down in the trenches,* so to speak, with all of the employees, and in particular, with all of the staff members from within all of the salons, be they just a floor assistant, a stylist, or a salon manager.

He knew them all, he had a way of being personable and concerned with all of them and their well-being, and thus, they gave him a tremendous amount of respect in return. He had no enemies or detractors in the company.

Being born and raised in Indiana, he had a core of staunch followers from not just the staff within all of the salons, but in particular, from out in the Midwest, since it was his home turf. Had the company let him go, it would have been disastrous.

He was like the Pied Piper of Hamelin, and in being let go and thus forced to start his own company, a massive number of stylists from multiple salon locations would have followed him in any new venture. That would have created an untenable situation that would have most likely eroded the total buyout value of the company in any negotiations, and would have compromised things in a major way.

That whole thought process of letting him go was canned almost as soon as it was initially thought of, and about to be executed.

Frederick had somehow gotten wind of what was about to transpire, and after he personally made the company hierarchy back in Los Angeles aware of what inevitably was going to happen should they cut him loose prior to the official buyout happening, there were second thoughts, and the idea was nixed before it was even put into motion. It had obviously *not been* well thought out. One of the things that it was probably predicated on was his initial dissenting vote to not sell the company during those board meetings when the devastating financial situation first came to light, and options were being discussed.

I think that in the big picture of things, it really didn't matter. As it was, the new Canadian-Euro conglomerate *owned both the ax and the chopping block*. At a certain point throughout the consummation of the negotiations and the final deal, it completely became their gig. It was irreversible.

Inevitably, in the immediate future, post-buyout, there would be any number of us, regardless of who we were or what position we had held, who would be terminated, and there would be nothing that we could do about it.

In the corporate world, it was the way things had been since the dawn of the business age. Indeed, it is the same way today, and you read about it constantly in the newspaper, no matter which sector of business or industry it pertains to.

Among my group of peers, all of us having been core employees, we would have had to have been *fucking idiots* to presume otherwise in our situation.

It was now a new year, and 1984 came upon us. The deal was finally signed, sealed and delivered, and the announcement was made to the press, as well as to all of the industry trade periodicals. With that, we waited for all of the final sweeping changes that we expected, and it came fast. *The barbarians had made it to the gate*, and they were swooping over the wall in droves.

I can't quite remember the exact timeline in which Frederick, Ron, and a few others who were above me had either finally been let go, or decided to simply leave on their own, but the ranks had dwindled considerably.

A number of well know stylists from London and throughout the whole of Europe had recently been brought on board by the new group, specifically to oversee national education for the newly amalgamated company, and they were making the rounds to do training at all of the salons. Quite obviously, it was a goodwill gesture by the new company to let us *supposedly know* that they valued that which they had absorbed, and that we should be self-assured about the future. To us, it was nothing but bullshit.

Truly, I think it was a smokescreen of sorts, to calm us all down, give us hope, and maintain overall tranquility, as further changes took place. Perhaps, what they were trying to do, was in the literal sense, attempting to give us all, en masse, the equivalent of a giant dose of *mental valium* spread out across all of the salons, so that we would just *stay cool*, and think the best of them as our new leaders. The fact of the matter was that I, as well as a number of others, was simply not convinced at that which faced us in the future.

The new group and its national and international holdings were huge, especially in the area of products manufacturing, which resulted in their earnings thus being in the hundreds of millions of dollars world-wide. In a company so large, I felt that my status had been reduced from that of live human being to then being nothing more than a computer number with a personnel file.

As far as I was concerned, I might as well have had a barcode tattooed on the back of my neck, and ankle chains binding me to my styling chair, only to be given bread and water every few hours.

I was in no mood to start over with another large company at that stage of my career, and neither were most of my peers in the company.

It became obvious to me, what I had to do, as well as where I had to go, and who would be there to support me in my endeavors. It was time for me to move on.

As the weeks went by, it also became obvious to the rest of my close personal core of friends and co-workers of the same rank that the new company felt no need for us. Little by little, as new people were being brought in for most of the key positions, it was now time for me to make a final and irrevocable decision.

There were few of us left by the time the carnage was over with, and we were essentially a ragtag group of stalwart limping soldiers, reduced in rank, licking our wounds, and heading to the nearest retreat, *but still waving a war-torn battle flag* that gave us identity.

It was over, but in so many ways, *we won*, simply because we were then released, and ultimately were able to pursue *that which we all did best*. In our loss, we were simply not aware of it at the time.

Fate is what fate is, and it is irreversible, especially when it is *fait acompli*.

I finally left the company late that fall, shortly before the Christmas holiday season, and moved to New York City with Meeka. My divorce from Maria had been finalized a few weeks earlier.

Because of my background, I was able to get a position working for a prominent London based salon group at their New York City salon on Fifth Avenue. I eventually made my way to their National Artistic Team, doing stage work all over the country. I stayed with them for almost ten years, and then went on to do national education, as well as further stage work at the national trade shows for a number of other prominent international companies. As of this writing, I have appeared at the International Beauty Show in New York as a platform artist over 20 times, until just a few years ago. I have worked with some of the top people in the industry, and I am very proud and gratified to call them my close personal friends.

Although I have survived two heart attacks and a minor bought with cancer, I am now semi-retired, and work behind the chair in a small but well-known salon in SoHo 2 days per week.

Meeka and I married a year after my move. She is a recognized editorial and fashion photographer, and has had layouts in many of the top fashion magazines, as well as having had much of her other work shown around the world at gallery showings.

We have two grown children, and a granddaughter whom we both love dearly. *She looks just like Meeka.*

We still do yoga, and are still very much in love. She is, and has been, the light of my life; my rock. I may no longer *be King of the Mall,* but I am very much *king of my domain.*

Frederick opened several highly successful salons in the Midwest. He is still cutting hair, still mentoring countless young stylists, and is still in my mind, *the boss.* He is one of my dearest friends in the industry, and perhaps the person that I respect the most. We speak regularly.

Gianni passed away....I miss him dearly.

A few of us kept in touch with Donny. Unfortunately, over a period of years, life has somehow gotten in the way, and we have lost touch with each other. I have not spoken to him or seen him in years, and neither have any of my former colleagues.

Reg went on to a study for, and receive, a Masters Degree in Divinity, and although he still keeps his fingers in our trade by virtue of working with Frederick a few days per week, he now has his own church congregation and travels nationally and internationally lecturing on behalf of his faith.

We have no idea what happened to Ron, the company General Manager. Rumor has it that he moved to Montana, left the salon business entirely, and is raising horses.

Maria married and divorced Andre. I had lost track of her over the years, especially after having moved to New York City from King of Prussia. A few years ago when I was back to that area for a visit, I bumped into a former female co-worker from the mall who still kept in touch with her. She related to me that Maria's marriage to Andre was apparently very abusive, (*as I would have expected*) and that in its aftermath she had a nervous breakdown which then took a few years for her to recover from. She had apparently moved to South Carolina with her younger sister, she no longer does hair, and has two grown daughters that she had with Andre.

Howard L. Schwartzman retired to Miami and passed away in 1999 from the MS which eventually ravaged his body, as well as the progressive nature of Alzheimer's disease.

I have *no idea* what happened to any of the women I slept with, or where they are…
…*Wherever they are, I hope they are as happy as I am.*

Milton Keynes UK
Ingram Content Group UK Ltd.
UKHW021823190124
436347UK00010B/656